THE GENTLE HUM
OF ANXIETY

Sarah Lee

ISBN: 1506187706
ISBN-13: **978-1506187709**

For Mum

"Just like a wandering sparrow,
One lonely soul.
I walked the straight and narrow,
To reach my goal.
God's gift sent from above,
A real unselfish love,
I found in my mother's eyes."

CONTENTS

SARAH LEE

ACKNOWLEDGMENTS

This book has been a long time in the making and would not have been possible without my rock, Jack. Who always pointed me in the right direction when I was about to give up. A big thank you to my wonderful F, who took time out of her busy schedule to add a little creativity to the project.

CHAPTER 1

It was the hottest summer Oscar Archambault could remember, mainly because he was stuck in Manhattan. Oscar loved Manhattan, but in the summer, especially if he'd been there for too long, he began to suffocate. *Too many people and not enough air*, he thought. It was the summer of 1939. The Spanish Civil War had ended; Hitler was invading Poland; Batman made his first appearance in a comic book; and *The Wizard of Oz* was showing on every big screen across the country.

Oscar lay on the crumpled white sheets of his bed, smoking a cigarette, unable to sleep due to the stifling heat. He listened to the early morning sounds of the Upper East Side from his open window. It was Friday morning, and he could hear the distant sounds of early morning rush hour on Park Avenue.

So far it had been an incredibly lethargic summer for Oscar. The first few weeks he had spent at the family home in Long Island, where he had squandered his days lounging by the pool, eating, and sleeping. When Oscar's mother, Iris, decided it was time for a change of scenery, she sent him to the family townhouse on Park Avenue, where he would laze the days away without being under her watchful eye. Oscar had just finished his freshmen year at Yale. He had gained tremendous praise by students and faculty for a short story he had written, which had been published in the *Yale Daily News* that spring. At the high point of the year, feeling immensely proud of himself, Oscar had told the paper that he planned to write a short novel that summer. He had his story and well-structured notes, but once the pen hit the page, it all started going wrong. Oscar fell out of love with his own story, and now he couldn't stand it. The thought of it made him depressed, so he avoided it as much as possible. He would leave the townhouse every morning to walk the streets of the city—never really going anywhere but simply going wherever his legs would take him. He always walked away from Park Avenue and the rest of the Upper East Side. That oppressive vortex, which lay within Fifty-Ninth to Ninety-Sixth Streets, always made him feel lonely. Oscar had never really fit into the world in which he was born, and the more he socialized with the Upper East Side, the lonelier he felt. While walking, he was able to escape the obligation of thinking about his writing, but his thoughts always came back to one thing, a girl to be precise. Anna Sterling was her name. He felt a gentle hum of anxiety in his stomach whenever he thought of her.

At the beginning of summer, Oscar had confessed his love for Anna at a dinner party hosted by his parents. She had smiled and walked away; that was the last time he saw her. He knew it was wrong to confess, but he had no choice. He truly felt his heart would explode in his chest if he did not express his true feelings. Despite the fact that she had a boyfriend, despite the fact she was his sister's best friend, despite the fact she was far too good for him, he had to tell her.

He was drawn to Anna the first time he saw her. He was ten, and she was eight. At first he resisted. He was a young boy who'd rather climb trees and ride his bicycle. Anna's mother had died when she was six years old. She was left with her father, Richard Sterling, and together they lived in his Madison Avenue apartment. Because Richard was such a busy man, Anna was either left alone or with her wicked aunt, Gladys Sterling, in Connecticut. Estella, who always got what she wanted, often asked her parents if Anna could stay over for the weekend, and so Anna spent a great deal of time at the Archambault mansion in Long Island.

Oscar remembered the first night Anna sneaked into his bedroom. She wandered in and sat in the chair by the window. "'I noticed that your light was on. I never sleep very well. Father says it's because I have an overly active brain," she said. "What are you reading?"

"*Peter Pan,*" he replied.

"Sometimes I wish that Peter Pan would take me away. I think I'd enjoy Neverland," she said, gazing out of the window. And thus began their story. Night after night, they built a friendship under the watchful eyes of the moon and the stars while everyone else in the house slept. Anna would sneak into Oscar's bedroom, and together they'd read, talk, and laugh until the sun began to show. Anna would then sneak back to Estella's bedroom and creep into the bed, careful not to wake her. She called him Oz, which he hated when it came from anyone else, but when Anna said it, it was just right.

Anna Sterling wasn't like any of the other society girls whom Oscar knew. She had pizzazz and vitality. She was adventurous and fun, and most importantly, she had ambition. Anna loved to dance, and ballet was her favorite. In 1934, she left Miss Porter's School and enrolled at the School of American Ballet in New York City. Oscar didn't see her as much after that, but he was happy knowing she was busy doing what she'd always dreamed.

Although thinking of Anna Sterling was a constant for him, Oscar knew he had to stop. Thinking of her gave him slight chest pains that he believed to be anxiety from the embarrassment of spluttering out that stupid word, *love*, to someone who has no interest in him.

Idiot, he thought as he rubbed the morning gloom

from his eyes.

Later that morning, in the dining room, Oscar sat alone at the long oak table, which would normally seat seven more Archambaults. Straub Archambault, the patriarch, would sit at the head with the grand window that looked out onto Park Avenue behind him. Iris Archambault, Oscar's mother, would sit at the opposite end near the door that led to the kitchen so she could keep an observant eye on what was coming and going from that door. Oscar was blessed as the middle Archambault child. There were six altogether: Sebastian, Johnny, Cornelia, Oscar, Estella, and Claude.

Oscar called the older the siblings the charmed triangle. Sebastian, Johnny, and Cornelia were incredibly good looking, fabulously charismatic, and extremely athletic. They excelled at everything they pursued. The charmed triangle were not only precocious, they were also best friends. Oscar was jealous of their closeness. He, Estella, and Claude were often excluded from most things that involved the charmed triangle. Oscar had absolutely nothing in common with Estella apart from the fact that they were both brunette. As for Claude, no one quite understood him. Claude was backwards. He lacked the ability to socially interact with anyone. Oscar believed that as the sixth child in a large family, Claude lacked care and attention when he was a baby.

Oscar looked at himself in the large mirror. At nineteen, he'd already grown into his six-foot frame. His dark, wavy curls were brushed back, forming soft waves across his head. He had his father's arched eyebrows and strong nose but his mother's soft brown eyes.

Justine, one of the young maids, entered the room carrying a tray with a glass of orange juice and a plate of grapefruit. "Morning, Mr Oscar," she chirped.

"Morning, Justine."

She put the plate and glass in front of him. "Your father shan't be home this evening. He's in Boston."

Oscar nodded while digging into the juicy pink grapefruit. The news didn't shock Oscar; Straub was rarely around.

Justine then asked the dreaded question. "How's the novel coming along?"

"It's not coming anywhere. I'm about ready to give it up."

"Don't talk nonsense. It'll pick up." She smiled.

"You're a real peach, Justine."

After breakfast, Oscar and his best friend, Augusten, played tennis on the outdoor courts east of Central Park. It was still early, and the sun had yet to reach its full force.

"Dammit! You know I've got a weak backhand!" Augusten shouted. Oscar knew his serves were too strong, especially for Augusten who was an awful tennis player, but he needed to let off some steam. "Why do you always go for my backhand?"

"To win!" Oscar shouted as he bent his knees, ready for Augusten's serve.

"It's getting too hot, and I'm tired." Augusten dragged his feet towards his water bottle at the edge of the court. He wiped the sweat from his chubby freckled face, which had turned as red as his hair.

"Have you heard from Anna?" Augusten asked as he flopped down onto the floor, trying to retrieve a banana from his bag. "Since the incident, I mean."

Oscar shook his head, trying his best to look uninterested.

"Sorry, buddy. I know you love her," Augusten

said and took a large bite from his banana.

"I'm over it," Oscar shot back. "She has a boyfriend, and I have Yale…and my novel." Oscar quickly attempted to change the subject. "I'm going to East Hampton tomorrow morning. You should come."

"Will Johnny be there?"

"Indeed."

"I'll pass. He'll just call us 'Oscar and the Whale' all night like it's the funniest nickname anyone ever made up in the history of nicknames," Augusten mumbled.

"Just tell him to back off," Oscar said, knowing full well that even if Augusten did stand up to Johnny, he still wouldn't stop. Johnny was a joker, a flirt who charmed his way through life, and most everyone adored him for it. The ones who didn't would never admit it to his face. Sometimes Oscar wished he could be more like his older brother Johnny, but then he would remember that Johnny had had his fair share of sexually transmitted diseases. Oscar couldn't see the point in chasing a dozen girls when he only really wanted one.

CHAPTER 2

After tennis, Augusten and Oscar went back to their houses. Both were sweaty from playing tennis and in need of a shower. Once home, Oscar walked from the en-suite bathroom into his bedroom wearing nothing but his boxer shorts; he sighed. At midday, it was already too hot. The wooden floorboards creaked as he walked towards his desk at the far end of his messy room. He pulled the chair back and sat, surveying his desk. At one end, heaped high against the window, were folders, exercise books, notes, and more books on various subjects. He'd bought the telephone from the hallway into his bedroom as he knew his mother would call at lunch time, just like she did every day. Oscar stretched his arms up and clasped his fingers against the back of his neck. He stared at his typewriter, which sat in front of all the clutter on the desk; it stared smugly back at him, as if knowing that Oscar would try to write, but that nothing magical would happen. The typewriter was a fairly recent addition, given to Oscar by his father as a present for getting into Yale. He adored it at first, but now he tried to resist throwing it out of the window.

Oscar knew that Anna Sterling was the reason for his creative block and the shameful feelings that grew in his stomach when he thought of that night at the dinner party a month ago.

After dinner, he'd gone into the drawing room with the rest of the men to drink brandy and smoke cigars. He'd caught a glimpse of Anna through the window. She was standing on the terrace alone. He excused himself and went out to her. Her long brown hair glistened in the moonlight, and her face brightened when she turned to see him standing in the doorway of

8

the French windows.

"Stand with me, Oz. The stars are so bright this evening," he remembered her saying. They stood in silence staring out across the garden, which seemed to go on and on before reaching a small woodland and then the ocean. This was Long Island Sound. This was where Oscar and his brothers went sailing and fishing, where they talked about girls, movies, and music. It brought back memories of a time when life didn't seem so hard. Oscar had always loved the ocean; it made him feel calm. He had grand plans of travel as soon as he finished his senior year at Yale. He'd think to himself, *That's all I need, the ocean and Anna, my happy place.*

He snapped back to reality and fed a sheet of paper into the typewriter, stretched his fingers, and lingered for a moment before writing,

Dear Anna,

How arbitrary of me to express such ridiculous feelings after three glasses of brandy. Please forgive my rude, and inconsiderate behavior.

Oscar Archambault.

He rested his fingers on top of the keys and dropped his head, laughing. He wrenched the paper out of the typewriter, crumpled it, and tossed it in the wastepaper basket. He fed a new piece in.

Anna,
I'd had a joint before dinner, which didn't

mix too well with the drink, hence my ridiculous outburst of love for you. Many apologies.

Oscar

Even worse! he thought and yanked the paper out. He chucked it, too, into the wastepaper basket. He fed in a new sheet and sat back. He pushed the typewriter back and grabbed a pen and paper. He began to write.

Dear Anna,

I'm not sorry for confessing the nature of my intentions towards you. I felt the time had come for one of us to lay our cards on the table. I haven't heard from you in almost a month, therefore I'm inclined to believe that your heart does not feel the same.

Oz

There it was. Everything he wanted to say staring back at him. *It'll do*, he thought.

Just as he began to feel the lightness of a tremendous weight being lifted, the phone on his desk rang. "Yeah?" he said after lifting the receiver.

"Oscar?" Her voice purred down the phone. It's was Anna Sterling. Only Anna Sterling saying his name could get the hairs on his arms to stand up. "Is that you? Why are you answering the phone?"

"I was expecting a call," he said, hoping to sound important. He wasn't about to tell her that the call he was expecting was in fact from his mother. He was waiting for her call to discuss what time he'd be at the beach house tomorrow and to tell her that Johnny was driving them up so she didn't have to worry about him catching the train alone. Iris Archambault couldn't understand why anyone would use public transport, because all she read about in the newspaper were muggings and death.

"I'm looking for Estella. Is she there?"

"No, she's in East Hampton." Oscar thought that she should surely know this. Estella and Anna were best friends, after all. He always knew exactly where Augusten was and what he was doing. Then again, there wasn't much change to Augusten's social calendar, unlike Estella Archambault, who was a social butterfly. She'd been in Paris with Iris for the first half of the summer, but unfortunately the trip was cut short due to Hitler's threats of invasion, and Iris's fear of war.

"Oh, of course. I forgot."

"You and your memory."

"Quite right. I'm an absolute goldfish!" Anna chuckled. "What are you doing?"

"Writing." *Why does she want to know what he I'm doing? If she cared what I was doing, then surely she'd have replied when I confessed my love rather than of leaving me to suffer with thoughts of impending doom for almost a month!* He thought.

"Of course, your masterpiece. How is it going?"

"Really well. The words are just pouring out of me," he lied.

"I wish I had your zest," she sighed. "I'm stuck in Connecticut with my aunt." Anna often moaned about what a hateful bitch her father's oldest sister was. Gladys Sterling was an aging spinster who lived alone in the Sterling mansion in Greenwich, Connecticut, with her two cats, Whiskers and Wilfred. She'd never liked Anna's mother, Maria Casillas. In her eyes, Richard Sterling was supposed to marry his third cousin, Katherine, whom he'd dated but didn't necessarily have any sort of connection with. Richard spent the summer of 1920 in Madrid, Spain, where he was supposed to be studying, but instead he spent his days hungover and his evenings drunk. One afternoon, while strolling through the Buen Retiro park, which he often did, he stopped by the monument to Alfonso to tie his shoelace. He looked across the Retiro pond and saw Maria. She was reading at the front of a little rowboat. A young man rowed, but that didn't bother Richard. At first sight, she had caught his heart, and he had to have her. He rented a boat for himself and rowed out to Maria and the young man. She spoke very little English but was immediately charmed by Richard. He took her to dinner that evening, and they fell in love. Two weeks later, they married. He then took her home, back to Greenwich, to meet his family, who thought Maria was OK but hated the fact their son had married a Spaniard and not Katherine. Not long after, Richard's father had a heart attack and dropped dead. Gladys, and many other women in the Sterling family, blamed Maria for the Sterling patriarch's sudden death and let her know it. Maria didn't care. She was in love with Richard, and that was all that mattered. Two years later, Anna was born, and their little family was complete. When Anna was six, her mother became very ill. Tuberculosis had attacked her lungs. The disease made her miserable, and her life became very black. She eventually killed herself. Anna found her hanging from the chandelier in the dining room. Richard fell into a deep depression, one that he was still not out of. Because Anna looked so much like her mother, Gladys seemed to blame her for the death of her father and the horrible sadness in her brother.

"It's torture," Anna said. "Do you know I'm so bored that I've painted each one of my toenails a different colour?" She laughed.

Oscar smiled. He imagined her sitting on a

large, uncomfortable bed in a plain bedroom that she occupied while at her aunt's. Anna often complained about the "dull bedroom" and how everything had to be kept neat and tidy.

"What colour is your right middle toe?"

"Blue."

Oscar smiled again. *She's the cat's pyjamas,* he thought.

"Oh, well. I was hoping Estella would rescue me. She's not much of a superhero."

"No, she's more of a villain."

Anna laughed. She shouldn't have—Estella was her best friend—but even Anna knew how completely self-absorbed Estella could be.

Oscar wanted desperately to save her from this boredom, from her wicked aunt and her horrible cats, from boring Greenwich, but he couldn't say it. *What if she says no or ignores me like before?* he thought. *I should stay at home. I have so much work today. But it's such a nice day. Why should I waste it sitting alone in my bedroom?*

"I can dust off my cape and rescue you, if you'd like." The words poured from his mouth. There was a silence. *Oh, no! Not again!* Oscar tapped his pencil against his forehead, a form of punishment for being so stupid and asking her to come to Manhattan to hang out with him, Oscar Archambault, who was nowhere near good enough for someone as perfect as she.

"I'll meet you at Grand Central in two hours."

Oscar looked up. His eyes widened. *Did she just say yes? Or some form of yes?* "OK, two hours; see you then."

She hung up. Oscar slowly dropped the receiver back onto its stand. He was dumbfounded.

Oscar stood in the shower, his second of the day, and it wasn't even lunchtime. He felt he had to have a cool shower because the phone call with Anna Sterling had made him all clammy. He needed to cool down, and a cool shower was the perfect remedy. He stood naked in front of the bathroom mirror shaving. He decided that he must look his best but not look like he had tried. Oscar had never cared about his appearance before; this was all new to him. It gave him butterflies in his stomach. He greased his hair and combed it back, whistling to the tune "Little Brown Jug" by Glenn Miller, which had been playing on the radio every time he switched it on. Oscar suddenly felt free, excited to meet Anna and spend some time with her alone. After all, things couldn't get any worse than they already were.

Oscar opted for navy blue trousers and complemented the look with a light-blue, short-sleeved shirt, navy bow tie, and white deck shoes with no socks. It was a brave choice but Oscar was already peeved about having to wear trousers instead of shorts. Straub would be appalled. He checked his breath into a cupped hand, grabbed his cigarette packet and lighter, and left his bedroom, letting the door swing shut behind him. He hopped down the stairs and shouted farewell to Justine and the other maids who were polishing various valuables around the hallway. Oscar exited the townhouse and smelt the fresh warm air before walking down the steps and onto the pavement to begin his journey towards Grand Central Station.

Oscar stood waiting in the main concourse of Grand Central, puffing on a cigarette, occasionally glancing at the clock. The bright sun beamed through the tall, cast-iron windows, throwing long shadows on the people who walked across the marble floor. He'd always been fond of the constellations of the zodiac that decorated the high ceiling of the station. This place always looked, to him, like an ancient temple rather than a hub for transportation. Oscar stepped along the cracks on the floor, trying to balance on the lines. He liked to test himself with these silly little games. Growing up with three brothers had taught him to keep a sharp head. When they were together, one of them would almost always challenge the others to some gallant task, and the loser would be made to do something awful. Sebastian almost always won. He was good at everything. This annoyed Johnny, and games would often end in the two older brothers battling it out while Oscar and Claude cheered their selected winner on. Oscar always rooted for Sebastian. He admired him despite the fact Sebastian had had a nervous breakdown when he was thirteen years old and spent most of that year in a special home in New Hampshire. This incident was never mentioned within the family and became an Archambault secret. Straub and Iris couldn't handle the humiliation of such a scandal. Luckily, after his stay in New Hampshire, Sebastian became normal again.

Oscar exhaled a river of smoke into the air when he suddenly saw her amid a sea of people. His heart began to beat faster, like it did every time he caught that first glimpse of Anna. She smiled in his direction, and he replied with a nod, trying desperately to keep his cool. She looked so free, like a bird or an angel. She was wearing only a light-pink summer dress and sandals. Her soft brown hair flowed loose. To Oscar, life couldn't get any better than that moment.

"Sorry, I'm late. Blame the New Haven Line."

"That's OK." Oscar smiled.

Anna grabbed Oscar's hand and began to unfasten his watch. "Today, there is no time." She smiled, slipping off his watch and sliding it into the pocket of his shorts.

"Drinks?" he offered.

"Sure." She linked her arm through his, and together they strolled across the marble floor towards the balcony steps and out of the station.

They found themselves in the Waldorf Astoria for drinks. Oscar rarely went there, unless it was for a luncheon with his father and Sebastian, but it was close to Grand Central, and he was too busy keeping his cool to be more creative. They sat side by side at the long bar sipping martinis. It was dark in the bar due to the deep red and dark wooden decor. "Why aren't you at the beach house with the rest of the Archambaults?" Anna asked.

"I'm writing. It's quiet at the house with father at work all of the time. Besides, I'll be going there tomorrow with Johnny. He wants to take his new car for a spin. It's a BMW Roadster, and it's fast, apparently."

Oscar watched as Anna sipped her martini. She stared back at him as she drank. Her deep brown eyes watched him closely.

Her eyes are sad, he thought. *They always have been*. All Oscar had ever wanted to do was make her happy, but he just didn't know how. To him, she was a mystery.

"Why did you bring me here, Oz?"

"I don't know," he said, puzzled.

"Do you think I like these kinds of places?"

"I don't really know what you like anymore."

"Anymore?" She seemed almost offended. "I'm still me, Oz. In May, I came here for my debutante's rehearsal. Partway through the waltz, I felt a tightening in my chest and a swelling in my brain. The

room began to spin, and I excused myself to the ladies'
room where I vomited." She lit a cigarette. "The idea
that I must wear a white gown to be accepted into
society so that some fool will marry me makes me feel
sick."

"It was foolish of me to bring you here. I'm
sorry."

"How could you have known? I often have
these feelings of panic. I've never told anyone."

Oscar placed his hand on top of hers. "Let's go
see a movie."

On hot days like that one, it seemed that
everyone in Manhattan ventured to the movies. It was
the only place you'd find good air conditioning. Oscar
and Anna sat side by side eating popcorn. Neither took
their eyes off the screen. They were far too engaged in
the story of *Dark Victory*. Anna leaned over to Oscar and
whispered, "I like Bette Davis." Oscar nodded, making a
mental note.

After the movie, Oscar and Anna walked to
Central Park where they lay on the warm grass of the
great lawn. He felt so peaceful he could have slept. Anna
turned to him and lifted her sunglasses above her eyes.
"Let's get a boat," she said.

Oscar sat on the wooden bench across the middle of the
little rowboat. He held the oars but did not paddle.
Instead, he watched Anna. She sat at the bow, her feet
dangling down and toes skimming the surface of the
water. She let her head drop back, and the sun shone on
her face. Oscar eyed her neck, wondering what she'd do
if he were to lean over and kiss it. *A rowboat ride in Central
Park is awfully romantic*, he thought. *It's a young lovers' game.
Is that what Anna was implying when she suggested it? Or does she*

find the soft ripples in the water relaxing?

"When I graduate, I plan to sail to Europe," he said. This had been Oscar's plan since he was a small boy. Maps and notes of his adventures filled his top desk draw. When Sebastian graduated four years prior, he took Johnny and a small group of friends sailing around Europe. Oscar was green with envy for the entire two months they were gone. Johnny spoke nonstop about the trip for weeks after. Sebastian not so much. Something changed in him when he returned home. It was as though he decided that the time had come to be a serious man. He proposed to his longtime girlfriend, Evelyn Bloomwood, and they had a beautiful autumn wedding shortly after. He then began working at Archambault Tower as junior partner and took lots of business trips to Utah to see how the copper mines were doing. Oscar would often say that Sebastian became monotonous after Europe.

"That sounds fabulous." Anna smiled. "And after Europe?"

"I'll sail down the Red Sea, across to India, through Asia and across the Pacific towards South America, and then home."

"Won't you get lonely?"

"I'm sure I'll make friends along the way."

"I don't think you'd ever come home. After that, why would you?"

"I'd miss things." Oscar smiled and lit himself a cigarette.

"Would you miss me?" She lifted her sunglasses and smiled at him. He exhaled.

"I'd miss you the most." It felt so natural to say the words that Oscar didn't even panic.

"Then I'd come with you." Anna let her shades fall back over her eyes and leaned her head back to catch more rays.

Oscar felt as though he was floating. This was the scene his dreams were made of. With a burst of happiness, Oscar began to row, and the little boat floated softly across the lake.

Oscar bought himself and Anna a refreshing lemonade from a stand on the Seventy-Second Street cross drive above Bethesda Terrace. Oscar came here often. He'd grown fond of the lemonade made by the elderly Jewish man who owned the stand, which was really just a wooden shack on wheels attached to a bicycle. He made all sorts of refreshing beverages—from orange juice to peach iced tea—but it was the lemonade that kept Oscar coming back. Anna agreed, although she admitted she'd be tempted to try the peach iced tea next time. Oscar recounted the time that his mother, in a rare domestic moment, made lemon iced tea and brought it to a luncheon hosted by Anna's aunt. Anna finished the whole jug before anyone else got to try it.

"My aunt gave me such a clout!" Anna remembered. "She went on and on about how undignified I was for drinking it all. She even complained to my father that I was not ladylike at all, the hag!"

"I admit it's a damn-fine drink. My mother can't boil an egg, but she certainly knows how to squeeze a lemon!" Oscar laughed.

They walked down the granite steps of the Bethesda Terrace and towards the fountain. The bronze eight-foot angel statue in the middle of the fountain was baking in the sun. Water cascaded down its body into the large basin below. Anna hopped onto the circular wall surrounding the fountain.

"This is my favorite place in Manhattan," she said.

"Look right, towards Madison Avenue," Oscar instructed. "Do you see that diamond-shaped clock stuck on that building?"

"Just about." Anna squinted into the distance.

"My great-great-grandfather, Claudius Archambault, made it. He came to this island as a penniless watchmaker. That great clock was his side project," Oscar said. "After he died, his son Maxim, had it placed on top of that building. Maxim liked to sit by the fountain and read. He always forgot to wear a watch and never knew when to be home for dinner. But this way, he could always see, and his wife wouldn't get upset, because he'd be home."

"It's so far away. How could he make out what time it was?" Anna asked.

"He carried a pair of binoculars." Oscar smiled. "Archambaults have many eccentricities. I had a great-uncle who used to row his canoe down the Hudson River in the middle of the night."

"Why would he do that?" Anna asked. She put out her hand for Oscar to hold while she hopped off the wall.

"I don't know." Oscar laughed.

"I've had fun today. Thank you for inviting me," Anna said, looking into Oscar's eyes. He could feel her gaze reaching in through his eyeballs, turning his blood warm, and making his heart pound faster. Oscar felt a warm wind whip and whistle across the back of his legs. Dry leaves began to swirl in all directions. Specks of dust glowed in deep sunbeam tints as dark clouds shuffled in the sky.

"Anytime," was the best he could mutter.

The air had turned humid. It had been like that for a while, but Oscar only noticed then, probably because he could feel his brow starting to sweat. Of course he'd been covered with a shiny coating of sweat all day but so had everyone else in Manhattan.

"It smells like rain," Anna said just as a few drops lightly fell.

There was a warm and wet sense of electric anticipation as lightning bolts flashed silently in the distance.

Oscar watched Anna's eyes and her lips parted, ready to say something. She muttered, "Oz, I—" but was interrupted by a loud crash of thunder. The sky turned grey as a loud roar shuddered through the sky.

Oscar jumped while Anna remained cool, not even flinching a little. The sky opened and heavy rain began to pour. Everyone ran, looking for shelter or a quick way to get home. Anna stretched out her hands and caught drops of rain on her palms. She leaned her head back and let the rain fall onto her face, just as she did with the sunbeams. Lightening lit up the sky. Oscar ducked and realized that they were completely alone.

"Anna! We should find shelter."

"Why? We're already wet!"

Oscar wasn't being fussy about the rain; it was the lightning that made him uneasy, specifically the thought of getting struck by it.

Anna grabbed Oscar's hand, and together they ran around the fountain, laughing. He kicked puddles of water at her, and she ran away. He chased her. The thunder crashed around them, followed by a lightning bolt and more rain. They didn't care; they existed in a world of their own—a perfect world where only they exist. They ran towards the lower passage of the terrace and took cover underneath. Oscar looked out towards the angel. Water was drizzling down her face and body before splashing into the basin. Anna looked at him. His curly hair was soaking wet. She watched the little pearls of rain run down the side of his face.

"I love you too," she whispered.

Oscar turned to her.

"I'm sorry that I didn't say it before. You surprised me." She was tearful, finding it difficult to speak through a constricted throat.

The feeling of infinite happiness hasd always been hovering between them. Perhaps they were once too young and innocent to know what this infinite feeling was. Oscar reached his hand up and gently stroked her soft cheek. He moved towards her so that their noses were almost touching. His lips slowly parted, and finding hers, they kissed. The taste of lemonade still lingered in her mouth. She pulled away as if taken by surprise. They had been childhood friends and now lovers.

After a needed moment to find her bearings, Anna moved towards him and kissed him again, this time more daringly—the tip of her tongue touched his. She sighsed at the realization that this *was* indeed the most natural thing. Everything that she hasd ever wanted had been right in front of her, in the form of Oscar Archambault. Anna's sigh seemed to have awakened something in Oscar. He held her closer, wanting more of her, all of her. He pushed her hard into the stone pillar. As they kissed, more freely now, she pulled at his clothes. He kissed her neck, softly biting her. He teased; she teased back by running her leg up the back of his calf. Anna pulled at his hair and pushed his kisses down her neck towards her chest and onto her breasts.

"Take me back to your room, Oscar," she

whispered.

CHAPTER 3

The optimistic outcome that Oscar envisioned while kissing Anna Sterling's neck under the Bethesda Terrace quickly changed. As he lay next to her, naked under the sheets, he was baffled and humiliated. He was Don Juan under the terrace, but as soon as they made it back to his bedroom, he had turned into clumsy Oscar Archambault, the virgin! Being a virgin had completely slipped from his mind until they got to the bedroom. Of course, Oscar had kissed girls before, but that was it. In the bedroom, he froze because it was unknown territory. He burned up while recounting the details in his mind. They had burst into the bedroom kissing. *That was fine,* Oscar thought. Their clothes were wet from the storm. Anna began to unbutton his shirt, and he unzipped his shorts. Anna then stood back and slipped out of her dress. He stared at her. Anna Sterling was standing in his bedroom in her underwear ready for him to have his wicked way with her, and that's when it hit him. The gentle hum of anxiety began to creep through his veins, getting louder as she moved in closer. She put her arms around his neck and nibbled his ear. *Keep cool, you fool!* Oscar kept reciting to himself.

"It's OK. The first time is always awful," Anna said, bringing him back to the present. "I don't mean awful. That was a bad choice of words."

The gentle hum was back. Everything was so perfect at the terrace, and then it was ruined. *Why didn't I listen to Johnny when he said, "Practice on the bad girls so that you're a stallion for the good ones."* he wondered. Oscar had never really had a chance to lose his virginity, and if he had, he probably wouldn't have taken it, because Anna Sterling was always on his mind. He'd managed to keep it cool until her bra came off. He just got too excited. Oscar had lasted roughly one minute and thirty seconds through actual sex, and then it was over.

Anna didn't look impressed. How could she be? It reminded Oscar of the time he went to see *Robin Hood* at the movies. It was great; he was having a hoot of a time; the action-packed movie was hitting on all six cylinders; and towards the end, as Errol Flynn's Robin Hood and Basil Rathbone's Gisbourne prepared to duel, the projector broke and couldn't be fixed. The end! And he didn't even get to the good bit. Oscar got his two dollars back, but that wasn't at all fulfilling.

He and Anna both felt robbed of their happy ending.

Oscar rolled onto his side to face Anna. He brushed her cheek with his hand and softly kissed her. His plan was to act nonchalant. *Just because it was a disaster on my end, doesn't mean she should suffer,* he thought. Robin Hood will have his victory!

Anna seemed to be enjoying the romantic kissing until she felt Oscar's hand slide down her stomach and towards her pubic line.

"No, Oz," she said, pushing him away.

"What?" Oscar replied trying not to turn red out of embarrassment.

"Not now. The moment has passed." Anna sat up and searched for her underwear.

"Reality always finds a way of ruining a good thing." Oscar sighed.

"What's that supposed to mean?" she asked, looking slightly angered.

"You should just go back to Ted if I'm so awful!"

"Don't talk about him! That's unfair."

"Unfair to whom? He's your boyfriend, and

you're here with me!" Oscar snapped. He got up from the bed and stormed into the bathroom, slamming the door shut behind him.

In the bathroom, Oscar grabbed a fresh pair of boxers from the drawer near the sink. He slipped them on and lit a cigarette.

"Fuck!" he shouted before punching the other door on the opposite side of the bathroom. This door led to Estella's bedroom. She had always hated sharing a bathroom with Oscar. He'd often hide rubber spiders in the sink, bathtub, or toilet to scare her. His crowning achievement was when he bought a rubber snake from Luna Park, which had a coiled spring inside. He curled the snake into the toilet and closed the lid. When Estella came into the bathroom, she lifted the lid, the snake jumped out, and she screamed the house down. She ran downstairs crying to Iris and Straub, telling them how awful Oscar was. He just laughed, even when Straub gave him a scolding, which angered Straub even more. Oscar knew what was coming. Straub took him downstairs to the study, stood Oscar against the fireplace, and caned him. Oscar didn't laugh that time, but he did feel that his punishment was worth it.

Oscar sat on the edge of the tub, smoking his cigarette and slowly bringing himself back down to a calm state. He shouldn't have gotten so angry, but he was embarrassed and vulnerable in Anna's presence. She insulted him and then rejected him. Finally, he remembered that she had a boyfriend, Ted Fitzgeorge-Parker. Ted was every girl on the Upper East Side's dream chap. He came from old money, much older than the Archambaults'. The Fitzgeorge-Parkers were in the oil business and were one of New York Society's most prominent families. Ted was twenty-one and studying economics at Harvard. He was captain of the crew, rugby, and football teams. He also served on the student council. Ted was the exact kind of guy that the Sterlings wouldn't mind Anna marrying. He was also the kind of guy who was well experienced with girls and would beat Oscar's ass if he found out what had happened, and if he knew what really happened, he'd spread the word and make Oscar Archambault a laughing stock. Sure, he was keen, but Oscar thought Ted was anything but a crackerjack. He'd always thought Ted was a dumb son of a bitch with the personality of a potato.

Oscar walked into the kitchen. Anna sat on a stool at the breakfast bar, looking into a glass of orange juice.

"Do you love Ted?" he asked.

"No," Anna replied without looking up.

"Then why are you with him?"

"Because it keeps my family happy."

"That doesn't make any sense." Oscar walked towards the refrigerator to get some orange juice. He filled a glass with ice and poured the juice over the crackling cubes.

"It might not make sense to you, but it does to me." Anna hopped off the stool and poured her orange juice into the sink. She watched as it swirled down the drain.

"Sometimes I feel as though I'm stuck in a state of numbness, and I feel hopeless. I'm drowning, trying to pull myself out of it, and then I feel the fear. The fear of ending up like her terrifies me." Oscar had only known Maria Sterling from stories and pictures. It was no secret that Anna looked just like her mother.

"My father looks at me with guilt and sadness in his eyes because I look like her. So he stays away. A gentle wave of anxiety comes over me, and I can barely breathe." She turned to Oscar. Anna clenched her fist and lightly slammed it onto the dark marble kitchen countertop.

"I'm constantly being told what to do and how to do it. How to dress and how to speak. Whom to date. What I have with Ted is an artificial relationship. Like I said, it keeps my family happy, and it keeps Ted happy because I turn a blind eye to his philandering. Plus, he lets me dance. He knows that when I graduate from the American ballet I'll be going to London or Paris and not a damn thing can stop me. Ballet is what keeps me going. It's that tiny light of inspiration that reminds me I'll be OK." She calmed down and forced a little smile at Oscar.

"And then you told me that you loved me, and it made me feel happy. Like you were always supposed to have said it." She reached for Oscar's hand and clasped her fingers around his. He moved closer to her and placed his hand softly on her shoulder, running his thumb down her neck.

"See yourself through my eyes, Anna. They're the only mirror you need." He gently kissed her lips.

Chapter 4

Oscar's eyes slowly opened. The sun blasted through the Venetian blinds on the window and stung his eyes. He rolled his head into the pillow, and then he turned his head, hoping to cast his gaze upon Anna Sterling. She wasn't there. Oscar stroked his hand over the sheet; it was cool.

"Anna?" he croaked, waking up his voice box. There was no answer. Oscar climbed across the bed and walked towards the bathroom door, which sat open ajar. He knocked and peered in.

"Anna?"

There was no one there either, not a sound, or a note. There was no indication that she was ever in his bedroom. All evidence of the previous night had disappeared. Apart from the faint smell of her perfume that still lingered, it could have all been a cruel dream.

Oscar, wearing only his boxer shorts, walked down the staircase into the main hall. One of the maids was polishing. She looked at Oscar and gasped.

"Have you seen anyone around here?"

"Anyone, sir?" She was puzzled.

"A girl?"

"I haven't seen anyone, sir."

"You've been here all morning?" Oscar snapped.

"As usual."

"Oh…" Oscar sat back on the last step. He ran his hand through his hair, trying to piece together the events of last night. The first time was awful. They'd fought.   They'd made up. She said he was the one for her, and they made love again; it was spectacular. Oscar felt more at ease and comfortable in her presence.

"Sir, are you OK?" the maid asked.

"I thought everything was perfect…why would she just leave?"

The poor maid was now even more confused.

"Don't worry. As you were," Oscar said, realizing that he had just had a case of the verbal diarrhoea.

She went back to polishing the woodwork.

His thoughts went back to their passionate kiss in the kitchen. That time their lips knew exactly where to find each other. Anna cupped her hand on his neck and stroked his ear lobe with her finger. He liked that.

"Oscar?" a deep voice croaked jolting Oscar from his daydream. "Why are you sitting here in your underwear?"

Oscar looked up to see his father, Straub, peering down at him. Straub stood just over six foot. He was a towering presence with broad shoulders. Oscar likened him to a brown bear standing on its hind legs. Oscar and Straub had the same nose, a strong Archambault nose, as it was known. They also had the same dark hair, only at fifty-four, Straub was going grey around the edges. Recently Oscar had also noticed small grey hairs in his father's mustache.

"How was your trip?" Oscar asked while standing.

"Fine, fine. Have you forgotten brunch? Johnny will be here soon. Get ready."

Oscar knew that Johnny was always late. The only time he followed was his own. He also knew that Johnny wanted some reefer for the weekend and that the guy he got it from, who lived in Brooklyn, never woke earlier than midday.

"He's late!" Straub exclaimed. Oscar quietly sipped his orange juice, trying to block out his father's complaints about Johnny. Oscar never understood why his father had so much negativity towards Johnny. Maybe he was jealous? Or maybe he just knew that Johnny could never be the suited heir to the Archambault throne. In the summer, the patio was filled with colours from the fresh flowers, which filled the warm air with a nice aroma. Oscar could feel the sun reaching through the surrounding buildings like warm hands on the back of his neck, like Anna's warm hands stroking his neck last night. He couldn't shake that shameful feeling of waking up alone.

"Let's eat. I'm not waiting," Straub shouted. He poured himself a glass of freshly squeezed orange juice. Oscar dove into the mouth-watering brunch that sat before him—fresh fruit and pancakes dripping in maple syrup.

"He's reckless." Straub complained. "He gets that from your mother's side."

The loud screeching of a car pulling to a halt filled the air. That was normal for city life, but Oscar knew it was Johnny. He always drove too fast, even when he should be slowing down to stop.

"Ah! Talk about the donkey, and it shall appear," Straub muttered.

Johnny casually strolled through the open French windows with a cigarette hanging from his mouth, his sunglasses neatly placed on top of his golden hair.

"I'm late. I know! It couldn't be helped." Johnny beamed. "I'm a fool. Father, how are you?"

"Agitated. We've started without you."

"Yes, I thought you might have." Johnny sat

down and stubbed his cigarette in the ashtray. He tucked into the food, wasting no time at all. "How are you, sport?"

"Stuffed." Oscar winked at Johnny.

"It's been a frantic morning. The traffic from Philadelphia was god-awful. I was sweating like a pig stuck in that car. I stopped by the office to wash up before heading over."

"I'm surprised that you even know where Archambault Tower is," Straub replied.

"It's the tall building downtown with Archambault written across it. Hard to miss." Johnny shoved a mouthful of pancakes into his mouth and grinned at Straub.

"You're junior partner, and the only time you show up to work is to wash up?"

Johnny nodded.

"You're lucky you have polo," Straub mumbled.

"How was the game?" Oscar interrupted, desperately trying to change the subject.

"Great! We won, of course. Freddie Masters managed to stay on his horse for the entire game this time."

Oscar chuckled remembering the time that Freddie Masters fell over his horse's head and landed in a great big pile of horse crap midgame.

"Boys, I shan't be coming to the beach house this weekend." Straub announced, tapping the sides of his mouth with a napkin. "I've spoken with your mother, and she understands."

"Does she have a choice?" Johnny replied smugly.

"Don't be difficult." Straub stood, and one of the maids rushed over to clear his plate. "Have a good weekend."

"Yes, you too, Father." Oscar smiled.

Johnny watched as Straub walked back into the house. "I expected this to happen." He turned to Oscar and lit up a cigarette. "I called the usual suspects this morning and arranged a little get together at the beach house tonight." He inhaled deeply. "And by little get together, I mean a huge party. Call everyone you know. It's gonna be the berries!" Johnny flashed a "devil may care" grin.

"Wizard." Oscar said sarcastically. The last thing he wanted was a party. Then it suddenly dawned on him that Estella would invite Anna because they were best friends. *Maybe this party isn't such a bad idea,* he thought. *If Anna is there, I can get some answers.*

"Don't be a wet blanket, Oscar! Are you going to eat that?" Johnny said while scooping some syrup drenched fruit off Oscar's plate.

The boys decided to leave straight after breakfast. The drive was long, and it was already too hot. Oscar took off his tie and jacket and threw them into Johnny's car. The white BMW Roadster was Johnny's pride and joy. He had fitted it with some sort of superengine, which made it superfast and superloud. Oscar didn't really understand the technicalities, but he liked it. He liked to feel the cool wind blow through his curly hair, and it did as they roared through the streets of the Upper East Side and onto the Queensborough Bridge, leaving the city behind. Oscar watched as the looming concrete jungle faded into the background before the three-hour stretch along the Long Island Expressway.

"We won't stop until we reach the ocean!" Johnny shouted.

CHAPTER 5

The magnificent Archambault beach house stood basking in the afternoon sun at the end of a circular drive. "Can you smell that ocean air?" Johnny shouted as the BMW pulled to a halt. "It clears my lungs and my head!"

Unlike the house and the townhouse, the beach house was not inherited. Straub had bought it after Sebastian was born. Friends asked why he didn't join the elite in Rhode Island, but Straub insisted that he didn't like being too far from Manhattan and that he liked the fishing in East Hampton better than anywhere else. It was only a two-hour drive from the house in Sands Point, but it was still an escape.

"You're here!" Cornelia Archambault came sweeping through the front door and onto the front deck. Her hair was auburn like her mother's and Claude's. The difference between the three was that Cornelia was the most easy-going person in the world. Negativity simply washed off her like water off a swans feathered back. She ran down the deck's steps and jumped into Johnny's arms.

"How was the drive?"

"Long and hot," Johnny grumbled. "I need to swim."

Oscar grabbed his bag from the trunk and made his way onto the decking.

"Oscar, why do you look so sad?" Cornelia asked.

"It's the heat," Oscar mumbled.

"He's all balled up about something." Johnny laughed.

"Lay off of him!" Cornelia teased.

Ignoring them both, Oscar made his way into the house.

Oscar dropped his bags onto the white wooden floors of the bedroom he shared with Johnny and fell onto the bed.

"Last one in the sea has to unpack my bags!" He heard Johnny shout from downstairs. He then heard the running footsteps of Johnny and Cornelia. They were both so athletic and competitive that most tasks were turned into challenges. Cornelia always won; Johnny always cheated; and Sebastian was always a sore loser. He didn't play games anymore, not since he married Evelyn. Oscar was excited to see Sebastian. He'd been in Martha's Vineyard for the past three weeks, and Oscar missed him. He thought he might ask his advice on the Anna situation. *Sebastian will know what to say. He's gifted with giving good advice,* Oscar thought.

Knock! Knock!There was a knock at Oscar's door.

"Yes?" Oscar shouted.

Claude, Oscar's fourteen-year-old brother, the youngest Archambault, peered his freckled face into the room. "Hi," Claude mumbled.

"Hi."

"Bye." Claude left the room.

Oscar shook his head and lay back down. He was used to Claude's oddball mannerisms.

Oscar knocked the door of his mother's bedroom.

"Come in," She called, softly.

Iris Archambault sat at her vanity bench, staring at herself in the mirror. Her auburn hair was tied up into a neat bun. Her dark eyes looked sad. At this very moment, she looked older than her forty -seven years. She saw Oscar's reflection in the mirror and smiled.

"Hello, Mother."

"Don't mind me. I had a migraine, so I slept in."

Although Iris did suffer from migraines, Oscar knew that she'd been depressed because of Straub's cancellation. Her eyes were red and puffy, and he knew she'd spent the morning crying.

"Do you feel better?"

"Yes." She smiled. "I shall be going back to the city this evening. The Drakes have invited me for dinner. Seeing as my original plans have crashed and burned before my eyes, I believe I'm free."

"Swell." Oscar was happy that she was going out because Johnny could have his party without having to dose her up on sleeping pills to keep her out of the way, which he *did* do the last time he had a party.

"I shall be back tomorrow evening." Iris stood up and placed an overly large sun hat on her head. "Please remind Johnny to pick up Sebastian and Evelyn. Their boat docks at six thirty."

"I'll do it so you won't have to worry."

Iris smiled. She placed her sunglasses over her red eyes.

"Good-bye, darlings," she said and exited the room.

Darlings? Plural?

Oscar looked round and saw Claude sitting cross-legged on the bed. He was reading the latest Superman comic.

Oscar sat on the shore, pushing his feet into the sand. He watched Johnny and Cornelia swim. He went out to write, thinking maybe some of the sea air would clear his mind. It didn't. His notebook rested on his knees, opened to on a page of doodles and drawings of fish.

Claude walked along the shore, carrying a bucket filled with sea shells. He sat down near Oscar. One of Claude's hobbies was to put objects in order of size. The toys in his bedroom were lined up across the floor, starting with plastic toy mice and ending with a large plastic dinosaur. Iris was forever rearranging her vases. Oscar remembered the time that Claude had emptied every cupboard in the kitchen and lined everything up in size order across the backyard. Oscar thought it to be a work of art, but Iris was furious. The maids spent hours putting everything back in its original spot.

"Hello, brothers," a voice called from behind. Oscar turned to see Estella strolling towards him. She, like Iris, also wore an overly large sun hat and big round sunglasses that made her look like a fly.

"Where've you been?" Oscar asked, not really caring what her answer was.

"Lunch." She threw down a sun mat next to Oscar and sat on it. Estella lay back, hoping to catch some sun before it got too late. "Would you tell Cornelia that her boyfriend has just arrived? I'd do it, but I don't want to shout."

Oscar rolled his eyes. "Cornelia! Bennett's here!"

Cornelia's face always lit up at the sound of Bennett's name. She'd only been dating Bennett Houghton-Knox for six months, but it was love. Oscar elected them as the perfect couple—one to match up to. Even Sebastian and Johnny approved of Bennett. Previous boyfriends had never stood a chance against their tricks and pranks, but Bennett shocked everyone when he passed all tests and not only swept Cornelia off her feet but also the rest of the Archambault family.

There was nothing special about the way Bennett looked; he was just average—average height, average weight, average face—the only interesting feature on his person was the small scar above his lip. Bennett would tell people that he got it from a shark attack, or a snake bite, or even a stab wound after saving an elderly lady from being mugged, but the truth was that he was born with it. He walked from the direction of the house carrying his shoes. His trousers were rolled up so that they didn't get covered in sand. Cornelia ran from the ocean and jumped into Bennett's arms, kissing every aspect of his head that she could manage.

Estella lifted her sunglasses and rolled her eyes. Oscar knew she was just jealous. Estella dreamed of finding her perfect prince, but she'd never been very lucky in love. She was dating Lane Hamilton until she caught him kissing some tramp from The Emma Willard School. Word through the grapevine was that Lane was trying unsuccessfully to win her back.

"Cute," Estella mumbled and got back to sunning herself. "Anna didn't call, did she?"

Oscar felt his heart begin to rumble like a bongo drum. At the sheer mention of her name, he felt faint.

"While you were in Manhattan, I mean," Estella said. "I told her I'd be back in the city, but my plans changed."

"I don't know," Oscar said, trying desperately not to give anything away.

"Of course you do."

"Nope, I've been busy."

"Right, with your writing?" Estella asked shrewishly. She could be very cruel when she wanted.

Oscar began to panic. *What is she getting at? Had Anna already told Estella? Is Estella playing a cruel game to bribe me for information? Or is she just taunting me?*

"I'm going for a swim." Oscar stood up and began to unbutton his shirt.

The water was freezing, but he didn't care. Once in up to his waist, Oscar dived under. He swam until he began to feel tired. People on the shore looked like ants. No one else was out that far. He pushed through the water with great strength, punching each wave like it was a taunting thought about Anna. *Why didn't she leave a note?* His head bobbed on the surface like a seal. Oscar didn't ask for much in life, but all he wanted—all he needed—was some clarity. To give him everything he'd ever wanted only to snatch it back was just cruel. He wondered what kind of monster Anna was and why he'd love someone so evil, so much. His overactive brain became so overpowering that he couldn't take it sometimes, not in a suicidal kind of way, just a mute sort of way. Oscar took a breath and let his head slip beneath the water, hoping to cleanse his mind of all the Anna malarkey for just a few seconds.

On the front lawn, outside the beach house, stood a large oak tree. The tree was the main reason that Straub picked this particular house on Lilly Pond Lane. The tree's largest branch hung over part of the driveway. Straub liked to park his car under it in the summer when it was too hot. At least he did when he came there. A swing hung from another branch. Straub had bought this for Iris on their second wedding anniversary. Carved into the wooden seat was the date on which they had wed—05.06.1910. Oscar couldn't imagine his father ever being so romantic. The swing was a gift from his heart and not from his pocket, which was a rarity for Straub now. According to Iris, her husband was incredibly romantic in the early days of their life together. He wooed her with roses when they first met, proposed to her on Sagg beach at sunset, whisked her off to Paris for their honeymoon, and treated her to a sailing trip around the Caribbean for their first anniversary. It was when the children were born and he had more responsibility within the Archambault company after his father's stroke that his romantic freedom began to die down.

Oscar sat on the swing, slowly moving back and forth while smoking a cigarette. He was freshly showered, and his hair was still slightly wet and swept back. He wore white trousers with his new brown loafers, a sky blue shirt with a red and white striped tie. In the hopes that Anna would show up, he planned to look his absolute best.

"Shit! we're late!" Johnny huffed as he barged through the front door.

No, you're late Oscar thought as he followed Johnny down the deck steps and towards Straubs car.

At the marina, Oscar sat in the car reading his book. Neither of them were late, the ship was. Oscar knew that Johnny was agitated. He wanted to get this over and done with so that he could start drinking.

Johnny leaned against the bonnet of his father's car. His crisp white shirt clung to his muscular torso., He didn't bother with a neck tie, just a crimson red and white striped sports jacket left unbuttoned. He flicked his cigarette on the floor as he saw Sebastian and Evelyn walking towards him.

"Greetings, brother!" he cheered. Not caring who heard.

"John, you old dog!" Sebastian replied, while embracing Johnny. "What's with the get up?"

Sebastian asksed, flicking one of Johnny's lapels.

"I'm throwing a little party. Hello, Evelyn."
Johnny kisses his sister -in -law on her rosy cheek.

"Now, when you say 'little' party?..." Evelyn
laughed.

"I mean monstrous!." Johnny smirked. He
took Evelyn's luggage and threw it into the back of the
car.

"Sebastian!" Oscar said as he embrased his
older brother. Sebastian stood a few inches taller than
Oscar, so his nose whisked past his neck as they
embraced. Sebastian always smelt like fresh laundry and
pipe smoke, which prompted a feeling of nostalgia in
Oscar's nostrils. "How was your trip?" Oscar asked.

"Swell. Not for Evelyn though. You know
how she gets seasick."

"Sebastian assured me that by ferry was the
quickest was to get here, so I decided to be brave."
Evelyn said as Oscar helped her with the rest of the
luggage. Evelyn removed her sunglasses so that she could
get a good look at Oscar.

"College has changed you." She smiled.
"You look enlightened." Evelyn leaned forward to kiss
him on the cheek, and he blushed.

Evelyn Bloomwood was once the prettiest
debutante in New York society. Well-established young
gentlemen across the East Coast wished for her hand in
marriage. Her bright blue eyes sparkled like the sapphire
on her engagement ring, and when they locked on your
eyes, well, it could make a crocodile blush. She and
Sebastian were like the perfect plastic couple that stood
on top of a wedding cake.

"Where's Father? I thought he was East
Hampton bound?," Sebastian asks.

"Change of plans. If he wanders too far

41

from the city, he'll choke on the fresh air," Johnny said. "Chet said he'll drive up."

"Van Laren?," Sebastian quiz'sasked.

"Of course. Who else? He should be here by eight."

"I thought he was in Chicago with Olivia?"

"Not at all. She's not coming, Didn't bother asking why. Trouble in paradise, I suppose."

"He's never really been tha—"

"Oh, leave it alone, Sebastian," Evelyn cuts in. "She'll get him back. She loves him far too much to let him go. I think it's rather romantic."

"That's because *you're* a romantic," Sebastian said kissing his wife's lips.

"I love you." She smiled. Johnny rolled his eyes, and squirminged at their public display of affection. Oscar laughed. He opened the passenger door for Evelyn.

"So, little brother, tell me about this novel you're writing. I hear you're the next John Steinbeck." Sebastian always knew how to make Oscar feel better. It was his gift. He always knew the right thing to say. Even when it was complete bullshit, he exuded enough charm to convince anyone of anything.

Claude was waiting on the porch when they pulled onto the drive. As Johnny got out of the car he whistled, to which the handyman came running out of the house to help unload the luggage.

"Claude, how are you, little fish?" Sebastian called to Claude, who was standing on the porch, eating an apple. Sebastian walked towards him and kissed him on his head, which was hidden under a mop of curly red hair.

42

"Don't worry about him. I'll lock him in the closet." Johnny smirked.

"Don't be wicked!" Evelyn shouted. "He can eat, mingle, and then I'll put him to bed." She walked up the steps to meet Claude and Sebastian.

"Claude doesn't mingle," Johnny called.

"Remember your wedding? He hid in the car all afternoon," Oscar replied.

"He'll grow out of it, won't you, kid?" Sebastian nudged Claude, who shrugged his shoulders.

Evelyn placed her arm on Claude's shoulder, and they made their way inside.

Oscar and Sebastian sat on the deck in the back yard. The sky had turned pink as the sun began to set. The house sat in the west, so no one ever actually saw the sun set, just the pink sky. Oscar didn't mind. He much preferred the sunrise. Anyone could see the sunset, but only a select few who rose early enough were treated to the magnificent sun rising above the Atlantic.

They spoke about summer and what had been occupying their lives over the past few months. Sebastian had mainly worked. He was busy within the Archambault company trying to get clients and coworkers to take him seriously and trying to prove himself as more than just the spoiled heir. Oscar desperately wanted to tell him about Anna and all that had happened the night before, but as soon as Sebastian stopped talking about himself, Evelyn and Estella came to join them with preparty martinis.

"James Danby just pulled up outside," Evelyn said.

James Danby, or just Danby, as he was known, was one of Sebastian's good friends. Chet Van

Laren was his best friend while Danby and George Brice took second and third place. Sebastian always said that Danby was selfish and that one should never trust him. "He's a good friend, but don't ever try your luck with him," he'd say. George Brice was an alcoholic buffoon and always made everyone around him laugh. Danby bullied George while they were at boarding school in Andover and carried on bullying him through their time at Yale. "Brice will probably die alone in a pool of his own vomit if he continues to drink the way he does," James would say before topping off George's glass with more vodka.

George, already on the juice, climbed out of Danby's tiny sports car. "This thing was made for dwarfs!" he shouted.

Sebastian laughed as he walked up the drive to meet his chums.

"You're just too fat, Bricey!" Danby laughed.

Oscar stood on the porch watching while Sebastian bear hugged his friends. Johnny ran out. "Porky! Danby!" he called as he made his way towards them.

Another sports car came speeding up the driveway. This one was bigger and carried more people —Johnny's rowdy friends.

"Boys!" Johnny called.

"Archmaster!" Charlie Barrow laughed. Charlie was driving; next to him was Sasha Chapin, Cornelia's best friend.

"Remind me never to get into a car with Charlie again," she said, stepping out of the vehicle. "My ears are filled with sand."

"And how lovely you look with sand in your ears, Miss Chapin," Johnny flirted, and kissed her on the cheek.

"Where's Van Laren?" Buckley Blythe, another of Johnny's friends, asked as he climbed from the back seat.

"I haven't seen that old dog all summer!" Buckley was heir to the Blythe Advertising company. When he was twelve, his father used him for a Moxie Cream Soda ad. His face was on billboards across America.

"No one has. He's off the grid, most definitely," said Richard "Dickie" Forrester, who was sitting in the back seat smoking a cigarette. Richard was training to become a tennis champion. It was rare that he was allowed out to parties. His father and uncle, who were also his coaches, were incredibly strict with ol' Dickie Forrester. They wanted him to be the best and nothing less. He wasn't really sure what he wanted; everything had always been done for him, and he'd never really had much of a chance to make up his own mind.

Oscar lit a cigarette as he wandered into the kitchen. He'd greeted the gang with a wave, knowing not to get too close or they'd greet him with a headlock and rough up his hair.

"Their train will arrive at eight. That's what Lydia told me." Oscar overheard Estella talking to Evelyn. "I'm not sure how trustworthy these things are."

Jonah looked up at the clock on the kitchen wall. It was seven forty-five. He stubbed out his cigarette into an ashtray and ran out of the house.

"Oscar!" Sebastian called as he saw Oscar cycling down the driveway on Claude's bicycle.

"I'll be back soon!" Oscar yelled back. He raced off the driveway and onto Lilly Pond Lane. The

East Hampton railroad station was a ten-minute drive from the house. Oscar knew that if he peddled fast enough, he could make it in eight. He looked at his watch—seven fifty. If Anna was coming to the party, she would be with Estella's friends Lydia, Julia, and Imogen. They were always together even though Anna was most definitely the odd one out. She wasn't as vain as the rest of them. While they all spent hours in Estella's room, Anna hung out with Oscar and Claude, either in the garden or the playroom. Sometimes they'd ditch Claude and run down to the small beach past the woodland at the edge of the Archambault's sixteen acres of land. Oscar kept his small boat tied to the little wooden deck. He and Anna usually sat in it watching the sun go down.

"It's my mother's death anniversary today," Anna once said, referring to her mother's suicide five years earlier. "What are you supposed to do with that?" She said looking at Oscar for answers. He'd never lost anyone before and didn't know what to say. He just shrugged and put his arm around her shoulders. She rested her head on his, and they sat in silence, bobbing softly on the calm spring waves.

He sped through main street, past the library and the church. He cut through the little park and past the school. Oscar arrived just as the train pulled into the station. He hopped off the bike and leaned it up against wood-paneled station house. The image of Anna walking towards him at Grand Central over twenty-four hours ago was still fixed in his mind. Groups of rowdy youngsters began to exit the train chatting and laughing; all were excited for the potential memories this summer evening might bring.

"Hi, Oscar!" a young man called; he was carrying a guitar. Oscar nodded in his direction. He was far too preoccupied looking out for a glimpse of Anna.

A few of Oscar's Yale comrades got off the train and waved in his direction. He didn't invite them. He didn't invite anyone; he never did. Johnny Archambault's party invites had a way of getting around.

Past his Yale chums, Oscar noticed Imogen, Lydia, and Julia. With them were two boys carrying a crate of alcohol.

"Hi, Oscar." Imogen smiled.

"Sweet of you to come and meet us." Julia purred sardonically.

Oscar nodded and continued to walk along the platform while glancing through each of the windows as he passed. Soon the platform began to clear. Most people had moved on, and the train was kicking up the engine ready to do the same.

Oscar sat on a bench at the edge of the platform. He kicked the pebbles of gravel beneath his feet. The train left and so had all the hustle and bustle. He was alone. The pink sky was turning dark blue and soon black. He felt entirely deflated and humiliated.

When Oscar arrived back at the beach house, the party was in full swing. Most were canned, loud, and annoying. Oscar needed to be on their level. He detested drunks, especially youngsters in excess. Chet Van Laren stood by the bar in front of the open French windows. He held a glass filled with ice cubes and a little whiskey. Chet was cool, poised. He held an air of serenity that no one else in the room did. Always immaculately groomed, Chet was never short of female attention, yet there he stood alone at the bar.

"Evening, Oscar. Swell party." Chet winked.

Chet was Sebastian's best friend. They had been so since they were bought into the world. Sebastian was born three days earlier. Iris and Margot Van Laren knew of each other on the social circuit and soon became friends after hearing their bouncing bundles of joy were so close in age. Sebastian and Chet stuck together through boarding school and university. Many were shocked when Chet didn't make an appearance at Sebastian and Evelyn's wedding. Chet sent Evelyn a large bouquet of white roses with a note explaining how he was incredibly busy trying to make a name for himself within the Van Laren shipping company and couldn't come.

"Drink?" Oscar asked and scooped a handful of ice into an empty glass.

"I'm set," Chet replied. He wasn't a big drinker, unlike the rest of Sebastian's friends.

"How is Olivia?" Oscar asked. He poured a little whiskey into his glass.

"We broke up. She gave back the ring, and that was that."

"Sorry to hear that."

"Can't be helped. She fell out of love with me." Chet laughed.

Olivia had been Chet's on-and-off girlfriend for years. She was from Chicago, and she was extremely pretty. She and Chet looked like they'd just stepped out of a movie.

Oscar watched as Chet's eyes moved towards Sebastian, who was outside sitting among Evelyn and her friends.

"I'm glad he's happy," Chet said softly. Oscar almost didn't hear. Chet finished his drink and dropped his glass onto the counter. "Think I'll go and mingle with the scrubs," he said before moving off into the crowd.

Oscar was drunk. He'd been sitting with a group of people of whom he could not remember the names. He needed some fresh air and decided to walk down to the shore. Oscar saw the burning colours of a fire in the distance. He decided to investigate. Johnny sat around a firepit on the beach not too far from the house. A small group was with him, which consisted of close friends and a few girls. Buckley Blythe and some girl were lying on the sand kissing a few yards away.

Charlie turned a wooden beer crate upside down to make a table. He put some tall glasses on top. Johnny poured a green liquid into each glass. He then placed a sugar cube on a spoon and lit it with a match. Oscar watched the blue flames fade. Before they did, Johnny dropped the cube into one of the glasses and began to stir.

He looked at Oscar. "Try this," he said and held out the glass.

Richard sniggered.

"The green fairy wants a little kiss." Charlie laughed.

Oscar looked at Charlie as if the brute were challenging him, coaxing him out as a chicken. *It's just a drink. Johnny drinks it all the time. There's no reason that I can't too*, Oscar thinks. He took the glass from Johnny's grasp.

"To the misadventures of youth," Oscar toasted before finishing the glass. He felt the cold, green liquid slide down his throat. It tingled, burned. Oscar shook his head and gasped. His eyes felt heavy for a moment.

Johnny quickly prepared the others a glass. They clinked glasses and shouted, "The adventures of youth!" and gulped collectively.

Oscar could feel a mustache of perspiration

form on his upper lip. The little green fairy was swimming through his veins, tingles following each stroke. He never felt more alive, nor had he ever felt more tired. He tried to stand up but fell back down. The others laughed. Oscar's legs tingled.

"Just let it take you, Oscar. Don't try to fight it," Johnny said.

Oscar lay back onto the sand. He felt the tiny rocks against his back.

"You always fight it. Just let go." Johnny smiled. He turned to the girl next to him and began kissing her.

"She told me that she loved me," Oscar whispered. No one was listening. The others were absorbed in their own hallucinations. "Then she left."

CHAPTER 6

He didn't remember much after that. He woke up on the beach cold and alone. Johnny had taken two girls back to the room he shared with Oscar. They were still asleep in the morning when Oscar went in to pack up his belongings. The two single beds had been pushed together, and three naked bodies were lifeless on top. Oscar left Johnny a note on the bedside table.

The train back to Sands Point was almost four hours, which gave Oscar plenty of time to catch up on some writing, but instead he slept.

"Port Washington North!" the conductor shouted, which woke Oscar up. Stunned he'd slept the entire journey, he decided to walk back to the house in the hopes that he'd wake up more.

The Archambault mansion sat at the top of a small hill called Half Moon Lane. From the front gate, one could only see a little of the roof; the rest was hidden by trees. Sebastian nicknamed the house Stronghold, a fortified place where each and every Archambault who had ever lived could go and seek refuge from the world. Standing five stories tall, with ninety-eight rooms on 6.083 acres of land, Stronghold certainly was its own world. The house was purchased by Phineas Archambault in 1890. A marble bust of Phineas's crooked old face sat on a plinth in the arched alcove at the top of the grand staircase. Every Christmas, Claude would place a Santa hat on the bust for decoration. Straub had never liked it but felt it'd be bad luck to remove it. Besides, if he ever did, his mother would have something to say about it. She regarded Phineas Archambault as a saint, and the day he died so did something inside of her. In her old age, Millicent would often speak of how Phineas had come down from heaven to have tea with her and read to her before bed. Straub would say that was impossible. "Phineas Archambault is six-feet under and then some." He'd laugh. They'd never had a very close father-and-son relationship though. Straub could never be a good father because he'd never had an exemplar himself.

Oscar spent the week absorbed in his writing, sleeping, and trying desperately not to think of Anna. Every time Estella received a phone call or a visitor, Oscar would suffer a miniature panic attack. Eugene Lynch, the butler at Stronghold, noticed Oscar's funk. Lynch had been working at Stronghold for thirty years, and as a silent observer, he knew the Archambaults a lot more than they thought.

"You're acting weird," Claude announced one afternoon. Oscar was sitting at his desk in his bedroom writing. Claude often sat with him reading on the floor of Oscar's closet. Whenever Iris was out, Claude sought the company of his siblings.

"I'm not the one hiding in a closet," Oscar replied.

"I'm not hiding. You are hiding."

"I'm not hiding anything. I put my heart on my sleeve, and she tore straight through it."

"Don't be silly. Hearts don't belong on sleeves." Claude chuckled and went straight back to his book.

It was a warm Sunday afternoon. Servants were preparing for the annual end-of-summer Archambault Ball, known to the rest of the country as Labour Day. Stronghold was overcrowded with tension, anxiety, and hustle. Everyone was in turmoil over the ball, as they were every year. Everything had to be perfect. The morning sun was already high in the sky and blazing down on the monumental facade of Stronghold. Oscar lay on the rolling lawns of the west gardens. He was far enough from the house that he couldn't hear the hustle and bustle. The only sound to fill the air was the dripping water of the fountain. It was so hot that Oscar felt tempted to jump into the green water. He'd ruled out the possibility of Anna showing up to the ball that night. Offspring rarely showed up to these kind of events unless forced by their parents. Anna's father hated these parties and never came. Oscar planned that he'd show his face, eat food, have a drink, and then make a sneaky exit back to his bedroom. Straub and Iris would be far too consumed by alcohol and conversation to notice. It was a foolproof plan.

"Morning, kid. Hot, isn't it?" a deep voice muttered.

Oscar put his hands in front of the sun so that he could see the face of the dark shadow standing over him. It was Sebastian. He removed his sunglasses and sat down by Oscar.

"What a nice surprise." Oscar was happy to see Sebastian, as usual. He hadn't seen or spoken to him since the party at the beach house. Sebastian had left midparty due to an awful migraine. "How's the melon?"

"How's that?"

"You left the beach house because of a headache, didn't you?"

"Oh, right, yes. I had forgotten. Oscar, that was so long ago. I'm fine. It must have been the heat. It always gets me." Sebastian laughed. "Evelyn's in the city shopping, so I thought I'd make a trip to Stronghold. Is Johnny here?"

"No. He went out last night, and I haven't seen him since."

"Typical." Sebastian breathed in the fresh

air. Living in the city, he didn't often get to breathe clean air.

"I'll race you to the beach." Sebastian smiled and jumped to his feet.

"It's too hot to run," Oscar moaned.

Sebastian shook his head and slapped Oscar across the head.

"Go!" he shouted before taking off. Oscar knew that if he didn't race, he'd never hear the end of it. Sebastian would tell Johnny, and they'd mock him all night. Oscar jumped to his feet and charged after Sebastian who was a few yards in front.

They ran down the green lawn and headed towards the woods. Sebastian dodged the tall trees and was closely followed by Oscar, who jumped over broken branches and boulders. Sebastian emerged from the green forest and onto the beach of Long Island Sound. He carried on to the shoreline, wetting his white pumps in the ocean. Oscar came up seconds later.

"Cheat!" Oscar choked trying to catch his breath.

"I was slow." Sebastian smirked.

Oscar hit Sebastian across the head and ran down the shoreline. Sebastian followed, now extremely fast. They sped down the beach until reaching shrubs and rocks. Oscar jumped over the rocks and up the small grass-covered sand dune. Sebastian followed. They ran for a few yards through the dead grassy dunes. Oscar stopped, panting for breath.

"I win," he called to Sebastian, who followed shortly behind.

"You didn't get back to the house."

"New rules. It's too hot. Besides, I don't want you getting another headache."

Sebastian smiled. His breath began to calm. He

rested his head back a little to catch the sea air. "How's your novel?"

"I'll kill myself if one more person asks about that stupid novel!" Oscar yelled.   "The truth is that I've fallen out of love with it."

"Something else on you mind?" Sebastian pried.

"Hitler and Stalin have agreed to divide Europe between themselves. Did you hear that?" Oscar said trying to change the subject.

"Of course I have." Sebastian sat on a patch of dead grass. "FDR will take care of us. That's what Evelyn says. She doesn't like to talk about war or politics."

"That's probably a good thing. Every which way you turn there's somebody talking," Oscar said sitting down next to his brother. He didn't like to talk about the impending war, not because he was oblivious but because it frightened him. Hitler was making his way through Europe, and it wouldn't be long before he made it across the Atlantic. Oscar knew that conversations about politics were important to most people, but he'd rather live in his own little bubble; things were bad enough there.

"It's important. It's good that people know what's going on over there in Europe," Sebastian said. "Americans are too self-obsessed. We think nothing can touch us because we're so big. Just you wait. It won't be long. Soon everything will change."

The brothers sat amid the long grass. Oscar fumbled through his pockets looking for his cigarettes. Sebastian took out a sterling silver cigarette case from his shirt pocket and offered Oscar one. The words *Always in my heart, together or apart. —E* were written on the top shell of the case.

"How did you know that Evelyn was the one for you?" Oscar asked lighting his cigarette.

"Because she told me," Sebastian joked, and then his face rapidly changed. It was as if something inside of him didn't want him to laugh, as though his laughter provoked guilt. "I think we just became content the moment we met."

Oscar smiled. That was how he felt about Anna.

"Even if the feeling doesn't last, I can go back to that moment in my mind," Sebastian said staring into the distance. "And I know that we were once truly happy."

"Only once?" Oscar asked.

"That's the repercussion of love. The punishment of searching for something that is long gone." Sebastian's eyes watered, and he became a mixture of sadness and anger. Oscar couldn't understand why. He knew his brother loved Evelyn deeply; however, he could sense a great sadness buried deep, a sadness that not even Sebastian could understand. Oscar was confused at the cause and concerned that he didn't notice it sooner. *Was Sebastian falling back into the black hole that swallowed him up when he was just thirteen years old?*

"Good things rarely last, Oscar." A tear fell from Sebastian's eye and rolled down his pink cheek. "It's so quiet out here," Sebastian said after a moment. They sat side by side in silence among the long grass. Oscar made of the gentle hum of anxiety hiss through the air.

Soon, they slowly walked back to the house, again in silence.

Oscar stood in the shower letting the cool water wash off the sweat of the day. He couldn't shake what Sebastian had said. It was a side of Sebastian that he rarely saw—the intimately tragic side. He wouldn't tell anyone. No one would understand, except for Anna, but he didn't plan of speaking to her for a while. *She can make the first move!* Oscar thought. He'd embarrassed himself enough.

He looked handsome in his black dinner suit. Oscar stood in front of the mirror by his bedroom window fixing his bow tie. It always took a second time to get it perfect. Straub had taught all four of his sons how to tie the perfect bow. The front window in Oscar's bedroom looked out onto the vast circular driveway. He could see cars pulling into the porte cochère. He decided he'd better go downstairs before one of the servants came into his room saying, "Master Straub would like you to come down to the ballroom."

Guests were entering the foyer and being led by footmen towards the ballroom. As Oscar came down the grand staircase, he noticed Sebastian and Evelyn conversing with guests. Sebastian was the prized Archambault son. He wore the mask of imitation well, so well that Oscar began to wonder where the artificial Sebastian ended and the real one began. Oscar put on a smile and greeted guests as he made his way towards the ballroom at the far end of the house.

The ballroom was beautifully decorated. The servants had done a splendid job, not that they'd get any credit for all their hard work. Praise for decoration would go to Iris for both the decoration and also for the wonderful spread, which she did not cook. Mrs Duffus and the kitchen maids spent all day in that sweltering kitchen preparing the appetizers for the evening.

"Apricot canapé?" asked a footman as he glided passed, holding out a silver tray.

Oscar took one and ate it whole.

A band played on the small stage at the far

east end of the ballroom. Back when Cornelia aspired to be a playwright, she had directed Oscar, Estella, and Claude in her plays on that stage in front of Straub and Iris. Of course, Estella would put on her best performance and turn green with envy when Cornelia received the adoration at the end of each play.

Oscar noticed Augusten and his friend Henry Overstreet signalling him to come over.

"Evening, boys." Oscar smiled.

"Oh, hi, Oscar," Henry grunted. He always had something to grunt about. It was never smooth sailing with Henry.

"Bee in your bonnet, Ol' bean?" Oscar teased.

"He's not great," Augusten replied.

"Not so great at all, in fact," Henry sighed. "I fell asleep in the sun yesterday afternoon. My back is burnt to a crisp, and to top it off, these callous brutes nudge my burn every time they ask me about Princeton! I'll scream in someone's face, Oscar. I swear it."

"Is that a promise?" Oscar chuckled.

"It's not funny. I spent the night in a cold bath and enjoyed it," Henry said.   "That's not something you're supposed to like."

"Why are you even here if you're in so much pain?" Augusten asked.

"Because my parents are sadistic assholes."

Oscar grabbed three glasses of champagne off a footman's serving tray as he walked passed. "Here. This will make you feel better," he said and handed a glass to Henry. He gave Augusten the other.

A laugh from over his shoulder caught Oscar's attention. He turned to see Johnny with Buckley and Charlie.

"Hello, Oscar, and the whale, and the other

one. Charlie smirked.

"You're no slim chicken yourself, Barrow," Oscar interrupted.

"What did you say?" Charlie turned to look Oscar in the eye. Oscar stared back at him. He wasn't afraid of chubby Charlie Barrow. It was about time someone stood up to him, and after the events of the past week, Oscar was feeling quite resilient.

"Calm down now, gentlemen," Johnny cut in pushing Charlie aside.

"Your little brother called me fat!"

"You *are* fat." Johnny grinned. "We're taking the boat out tomorrow for one last sail before summer ends. Care to join?"

It was an odd thing for Johnny to invite Oscar to events.

"One last drift?" Sebastian appeared. Sailing was Sebastian's favorite recreation. It was no surprise that his large ears overheard that part of the conversation from a few feet away. "Count me in."

Oscar looked towards Henry and Augusten. There was no chance they'd ever want to be stuck on a boat with Charlie Barrow, or any of Johnny's cronies for that matter. "We're having our own drift," Oscar said. "But thanks."

"Suit yourself, sport." Johnny shrugged.

As the boys settled into a heated conversation about sailing, Oscar's eyes began to wander the room out of boredom. Henry and Augusten had made their way towards a plate of cranberry feta pinwheels. *I'll join them soon enough*, Oscar thought. Mrs Duffus's special appetizers always won in Oscar's stomach, which turned as his eyes caught site of Ted Fitzgeorge-Parker. Oscar felt queasy. He felt his head turn warm. Of course, Anna was standing next to Ted.

He was tall and handsome, and Anna came to his shoulder. He was smart in a black dinner suit. She looked beautiful in pale blue. *Why is she here!* Oscar thought. *Was this some part of a savage plan to torture me? Boy, it sure is working.* He was angry with her—angry for leaving him, angry for not calling him, and angry for showing up to *his* house with stupid Ted Fitzgeorge-Parker.

Anna looked towards him as though she knew he was there. She'd obviously spotted him long before he had her and had kept her eye on his whereabouts.

Footman Jenks appeared at Sebastian's side. "Mr Van Laren is here to see you, sir" he whispered.

"Chet's here?" Johnny asked. "Bring that ol' cad in here!"

"Not to worry. I'll go and see what's keeping him." Sebastian left the circle hastily.

"It's been so long since I've seen Van Laren," Buckley announced. "Where's he been all summer?"

"He was at the beach house last week." Surely Oscar didn't imagine Chet's presence at the party. He'd spoken to him before any absinthe was consumed.

"No, he wasn't," Charlie said. No one really cared whether Chet was at the party or not. They were quick enough to jump onto the subject of how stunning Tilly Davis looked in the satin green dress she was wearing. Johnny excused himself and made his way towards Tilly before Buckley got the chance. Charlie wasn't yet drunk enough to be able to talk to women, so he stayed behind. Charlie only really ever got lucky when the girl was just as drunk.

Oscar looked back towards Anna, who'd now moved. All he could see was Ted making his way towards Buckley and Charlie. Oscar scoped the room hurriedly. He caught a glimpse of Anna moving through the white drapes, which covered the open French windows. Oscar made his way through the crowd and then through the French window out onto the south terrace. Anna stood under the stars. Oscar made his way towards her.

"Why are you here?" He didn't think. It was rude, but he was passed being courteous.

"Estella invited me." She lit a cigarette.

"You shouldn't have come."

"Oh, don't be so dramatic." She purred exhaling a river of smoke in his direction.

"I'm not being dramatic!" Oscar snapped. "You left. Without a word!"

"Keep your voice down," Anna said looking around the terrace. There weren't many people around to hear, especially at that side of the terrace, but Anna didn't like Oscar shouting at her.

"And now you're here! In my house! With him!" Oscar lowered his voice. He'd not realized how loud he'd gotten.

"Where's your decency?"

Now that he'd unleashed the anger, Oscar felt sad. She was standing here right in front of him and all he wanted to do was to hold her.

"Where's *your* sense of adventure?" Anna smiled.

Oscar couldn't play a game, not with this situation, anyway. His love for her was vast and deep within him. It hurt that she wanted to play with his feelings.

"It broke my heart when you left," he said quietly, trying to hold back at least a little.

"I'm no good for you, Oz." Anna raised her hand and gently stroked Oscar's warm cheek. He turned away. Oscar couldn't have any of her unless it was all of her.

"Yes, you are."

"I'm sorry."

"No, you're not," he muttered sadly. He needed a strong drink. He had to get away from Anna before she noticed how truly heartbroken he was. He'd already embarrassed himself enough. The gentle hum of anxiety was back. It had been masked by anger before, but now he could feel it in the pit of his stomach.

They were interrupted by a variety of voices. Ted, Johnny, Buckley, Cornelia, and Bennett were making their way out onto the terrace.

"Sweetheart," Ted smiled making his way towards Anna. "Archambault has some reefer." He kissed her cheek.

"Indeed I do. Join us for a quick smoke in the woods?" Johnny smiled.

"Yes, sounds like fun," Anna replied.

"I'm not going," Cornelia said. "We just came out for some fresh air." Bennett put his arm around her shoulders. She snuggled into his chest.

"Oscar?" Johnny pressed.

"No," Oscar said before making his way back into the ballroom. He needed that drink, and he needed to be away from people. The gentle hum was slowly getting louder. He could feel it pulsating within him. As he made his way through the ballroom, he hoped that no one would stop and speak with him. Oscar felt the urge to punch something—preferably Ted's face—but his pillow would have to suffice.

He came from the ballroom uninterrupted. *Thank Christ!* He thought. Oscar made his way down the dimly lit east hallway. There was less chance of him running into anybody this way, as guests were always led to the ballroom via the western hallway. The east was saved for the servants as it was closer to the staircase leading down to the ground floor where the kitchen and servants' quarters were. It also led to the second staircase, so Oscar wouldn't have to use the grand staircase; he'd surely be noticed if he used that. The staircase was hidden down a dark passageway beside the double oak doors that led into the library. As he passed, Oscar noticed light under the double doors. It struck him as odd because Straub always made sure that the library was locked during parties. The room doubled as Straub's study, and he didn't like anyone snooping around. It was common for guests to curiously wander great houses like these, and Straub was a man who always took precautions.

Curiosity took hold of Oscar, and he veered from the staircase and towards the oak doors. Pushing them open a little, he popped his head into the dark room, which was always dark because the thick red drapes didn't let much light in. Everything from the floors to the walls to the bookshelves was wooden oak, which wasn't exactly the lightest of material. This room always reminded Oscar of his father. It faintly smelt of wood and cigar smoke, and Straub spent the majority of his time in here, either at the desk or the leather chair by the window, which one could see the ocean from.

He noticed two shadows across the room; two figures standing close by the window were lit up by the moonlight outside. Oscar peered in farther to see who they were. The couple was passionately kissing. If Straub knew there was necking going on in his study, he'd be as mad as a hornet. The figures pulled away from each other. Oscar gasped. In the light he could make out Sebastian's face. He was kissing someone else —someone who wasn't Evelyn! *How could he do such a thing?* Oscar thought. He tried to see who the other occupant was, but it was too dark. But soon enough, the other face moved into the light and planted a kiss on Sebastian's lips. The gentle hum had frozen; everything stopped cold within Oscar's body. It was Chet Van Laren. Oscar stood there stupidly, not knowing what to do. He slowly backed out of the room hoping to erase the image from his mind.

"Watch your step, sport." Oscar turned suddenly upon hearing the familiar voice. Johnny stood in front of him.

"I need a flashlight," Johnny said. Oscar stared at him for a moment before fumbling through his pockets looking for a cigarette lighter. He thought that might make a good enough substitute, but of course, his pockets were empty. "There's a flashlight in the kitchen. Mrs Duffus will let you use it." Oscar panicked.

"Move aside. Father has one in the drawer." Johnny tried nudging Oscar out of the way, but he resisted. Oscar stared Johnny in the eye and turned his body into stone so that his older brother couldn't get passed.

"I'll knock you on your ass, Oscar!" Johnny said beginning to feel threatened.

Oscar stared at him weighing out his options but unable to think clearly. He knew that Johnny would find a way into the room eventually. Oscar lowered his head in defeat and stepped to the side, allowing Johnny full access to the double doors. Johnny raised his eyebrows and nodded at Oscar. "Good boy," he said in his superior tone that was like a second language to him.

Oscar watched his brother enter the library.

He contemplated disappearing upstairs. He felt weak.

Sebastian pushed Chet away from him as soon as he heard footsteps over by the door. Johnny moved into their view, when he was standing by the desk. He turned the lamp on.

"What's going on in here?" Johnny asked.

Oscar stood quietly next to Johnny. He looked to Sebastian, who was as pale as a ghost.

"Nothing. Chet and I were just talking. Drink?" Sebastian made his way towards his brothers. Johnny stared at Chet like a bull preparing to charge. Oscar could see the anger rising inside of Johnny.

"I was just leaving," Chet said straightening his hair back into place.

Sebastian panicked. He tried desperately to convince Johnny and Oscar that it was all a big misunderstanding, but they'd seen it with their own eyes, and one cannot falsify what someone has seen for themselves.

"I'm no fool. I saw you," Johnny said.

"You don't know what you're talking about," Sebastian replied restlessly.   "You didn't see anything." Sebastian looked at Oscar hoping that he'd say something to end the whole situation, hoping that he'd convince Johnny to forget it.

"I saw you with Chet," Oscar said.

"This is bullshit." Chet was getting agitated. He marched towards the doorway, pushing Johnny as he passed. Johnny grabbed him by the elbow and pulled him back into the middle of the room.

"Just drop it, John," Chet said.

"I can't!" Johnny shouted before punching Chet in the face and knocking him onto the couch. Johnny began to pace like a boxer in front of a bewildered opponent. Johnny kicked Chet in the stomach over and over before Sebastian grabbed him and pulled him away.

"Don't you fucking touch me. You make me sick. Both of you!" Johnny said before lunging at Sebastian and knocking him in the face with his elbow. Johnny crawled on top of Sebastian and began to punch him using both fists, one after the other. Sebastian began to cry.

"I'm sorry. I'm sorry," he shouted over and over.

Chet pulled Johnny off Sebastian. Oscar couldn't just stand there helplessly watching. He pushed Chet away, which allowed Johnny the freedom to kick Sebastian.

"Oscar, stop!" Chet shouted. Oscar pushed him again.

"You saw it too, Oscar!" Johnny screamed. "How can you not want to kill that fag!"

Oscar was angry, but possibly more confused. He hated Chet at that moment, but he did not want to see him killed. He wasn't as aggressive as Johnny. Oscar worked with reason whereas Johnny worked with fists. He hoped that beating the guilt from Sebastian would work, and Oscar should do the same with Chet.

Sebastian stumbled to his feet and charged at Johnny, knocking him into a bookshelf. Sebastian was no longer weak; he was furious. He began to punch the life out of Johnny, taking out all of his anger and aggression on his face. Johnny fought back, of course, giving as good as he got. They often fought, especially as kids, but nothing like this. There was so much hate. Blood began to pour from each of their noses. Johnny grabbed Sebastian by the head and spun him into the French windows. The glass shattered all around, and Sebastian flew out onto the terrace.

Because the library was near the ballroom, they both shared the south terrace. Sebastian and Johnny's bodies flew through the French windows and caught the attention of the few guests who were out on the terrace. Sebastian stumbled down the steps and onto the lawn to keep out of view of people. Johnny followed with clenched fists.

"This is all your fault," Oscar shouted at Chet as they ran down the steps. Oscar grabbed the lapels of Chet's black dinner jacket. He felt the urge to hit him. He had ruined Sebastian's life. Oscar felt a pair of large hands on his shoulders pulling him away from Chet. It was Bennett. "What's going on here?" he asked.

Cornelia ran over after Bennett. "Oh, God!" she screamed, looking towards Johnny and Sebastian. "They're going to kill each other!" She tried to split them up, but Bennett pulled her back before she had a chance.

Bennett tried to grab Johnny to hold him back. Oscar grabbed Sebastian. He was strong, but Oscar used all of his strength to overpower him.

"Stop it! Stop it!" Cornelia screamed as Johnny broke free of Bennett's grip and continued to pound Sebastian's face. Sebastian tried to kick Johnny off while Oscar pulled him back. Buckley dashed over and helped Oscar pull Sebastian away.

Evelyn, Estella, and a few others came running out after being alerted to the drama.

"Sebastian!" Evelyn screamed as soon as she saw the chaos on the lawn.

"Do something!" Estella shouted at Chet. There was nothing he could do because he'd already done enough. Chet was afraid.

"I hate you, bastard!" Johnny shouted as Bennett pulled him back—this time with the help of Lane. "You make me sick!"

"What the hell is going on here!" Straub roared as he came marching out onto the lawn. A panic-stricken Iris followed.

"He's a fag!" Johnny shouted.

"I'm not! I'm not!" Sebastian cried.

"I saw him with Chet. They're queers, both of them!" Johnny bellowed towards Straub.

Sebastian began to vomit on the lawn. Chet pushed his way passed the crowd and made a swift exit.

"It's not my fault. I'm sorry. I'm sorry," Sebastian said over and over between heaves. "Mother." He wept, looking towards Iris.

"No, Iris," Straub said as he saw Iris move towards her devastated son. "Everyone back inside!" He motioned a signal to the footman who began leading the guests back into the house.

Johnny stormed back into the house followed by his cronies. He stopped in front of Evelyn. "I'm sorry. You deserve better," he whispered before carrying on back to the house.

Cornelia hugged Sebastian, trying to help him. Sebastian just pushed her away. He was in a state and wanted no one near him. Bennett pulled her back and led her to the house.

"Oscar, back inside," Straub said.

Oscar rushed into Cornelia's bedroom. He didn't turn on the light. From her bedroom window, he could see Straub and Sebastian if they were still out on the lawn. They were. Sebastian was trying to speak with his father but was interrupted by heaves and coughs. Straub kept his distance. Any normal father would comfort his son if he was in such distress—but not Straub. Oscar didn't know whether he believed what Johnny had said, but the comment was announced to all who could hear. Johnny had said *fag* and *queer.* Two words Straub Archambault would certainly not like associated with anyone in his family, especially his oldest son, Sebastian.

Oscar could hear the sound of Straub's muffled shouts. He pointed at Sebastian. Sebastian then ran back into the house. "Get out!" Straub shouted, louder this time.

Oscar ran out of Cornelia's bedroom. Across the hall at the top of the staircase, he could see Sebastian and Evelyn leaving through the front door.

"Sebastian!" Oscar shouted. He ran down the staircase, across the entrance hall, and outside.

Sebastian and Evelyn got into their chauffeured limousine.

"Sebastian! Wait!" Oscar shouted. He ran towards the car, which moved down the driveway. The car began to pick up speed as it neared the open gate. Oscar ran faster. "Sebastian!" He shouted again, hoping that the car would stop. It didn't; instead it drove down the hill and into the darkness. Oscar gave up. He was out of breath. Guilt washed over him. He wanted to apologize to Sebastian. It was all his fault. He moved aside and let Johnny into the library knowing full well what he'd see.

As Oscar made his way back to the house, he noticed that Cornelia, Estella, and Claude were standing outside the porte cochère.

"Has he gone?" Cornelia asked. Oscar nodded.

"He should stay away, at least for a while," Estella said.

"He's still our brother, Estella." Oscar snapped.

"Rich, coming from you." She smirked.

Oscar pushed passed her and went back into the house.

A jolt within sleep awoke Oscar. He sat up in bed. Cornelia stood in the darkened doorway, her skin pale and eyes red.

"Sebastian's dead," she whispered through a tearful rasp. "He's killed himself."

As Oscar made his way into the foyer, he heard loud screams coming from the drawing room. Lynch stood by the door with his head lowered.

"My boy! Not my boy!" Iris bawled.

She was lying on the floor in Straub's arms. Her maid, Miss O'Barry, stood next to Straub, trying to console Iris. Oscar looked at his father, who'd always looked so powerful, but at that moment was completely shattered. He held Iris's head next to his and whispered, "It's going to be OK. It's going to be OK."

Oscar moved towards Estella and Claude, who stood in the corner of the room. Estella was crying. She held her hand over her mouth as though she were trying to hide it. Seeing her mother this way was clearly breaking Estella's heart.

"Where's Johnny?" Oscar whispered.

"He ran away," Claude replied.

Oscar ran across the lawn, through the early morning mist, and headed towards the woods. He knew that Johnny would be at the dock. He charged through branches, just like he had done not even twenty-four hours before when racing Sebastian. He ran over leaves and forest rubble; he jumped over the fallen tree. Once on the beach, he saw Johnny standing at the edge of the dock and watching the sun rise over Long Island Sound.

Oscar was breathless. He felt the tears pour

down his face. He finally let go of the stupor he'd been numbly holding onto since Cornelia had told him about Sebastian. He loved Sebastian and hoped that Sebastian knew this in spite of what had happened last night. Oscar didn't care if Sebastian loved Chet Van Laren; he just wanted him to be happy because in the end that was all that mattered.

The days leading up to Sebastian's funeral were a blur for Oscar. Iris spent her days weeping in bed. Estella often lay with her. Straub locked himself away in the library. He did not like to speak about Sebastian or the events that took place on that fateful evening of the Archambault end-of-summer ball. Johnny left. His boat was gone. Everyone assumed that he'd return for the funeral, but he didn't. With a heavy heart, Straub wrote Johnny a letter telling him how appalled he was that Johnny had left his family at a time when they needed him most. He also told him he'd never be able to forgive him for not attending the funeral. The letter was to be mailed as soon as he had an address to send it. Evelyn focused all of her energy on the planning of the funeral. No one knew what had happened between Sebastian and Evelyn after the party. Oscar guessed that she had gone to bed and left Sebastian alone. He'd been so ashamed of what had happened between Chet and him —and so distraught that people knew—that Oscar imagined his mind was already made up. He saw it in Sebastian's eyes as soon as Johnny told Straub, and he saw the change in how he looked at him. Sebastian was no longer his pride and joy. He was an embarrassment. He disgusted him. It was at that moment Sebastian must have felt he had no other choice but to take his own life. Of course, Oscar didn't notice it at the time; it was only by recounting the series of events over and over in his head that he could come to that conclusion.

Unable to admit their grief—let alone share it—the Archambaults mourned in inarticulate loneliness. Iris rarely left the house, and when she did, it was to walk her two dachshunds along the beach. Straub spent his days at Archambault Towers in the city and his evenings alone. He hid away in the library listening to Wagner and drinking himself to sleep, devastated that his hopes for Sebastian were gone. Estella went back to school, as did Cornelia. Everything seemed to be broken, and there was no way of fixing it. Oscar was glad to be going back to Yale. Stronghold was keeping a strong hold on his depression. He knew he had to get out of there.

Oscar hadn't heard from Anna, not that he expected to. After all, she told him that there was nothing between them. He decided that she had no business in his life anymore. It was a sad thought, but he just couldn't long for her anymore. It was too upsetting for him, especially at that time. Back at his Yale lodgings, he entered the communal common room and dropped his bags at the door. He shared this room with six other boys. Each had their own dorm rooms that branched off the communal room. Oscar's was at the far end, near the window. He went to unlock his door, but someone had beaten him to it. *An intruder?* he wondered. He felt around for the spare key above his doorframe, but it was gone. One of his roommates must have locked themselves out and needed a place to crash.

"OK, what's the big idea?" he bellowed as he pushed open the door, hoping to catch the intruder off guard.

Oscar froze upon seeing Anna sitting on his bed. She turned to look at him; her eyes were red. She'd been crying or was about to.

"I'm sorry about Sebastian," she said. "I'm sorry that I wasn't there for you." She stood up and slowly moved towards Oscar. "I *do* love you, very much. I'm sorry I told you otherwise. I was just afraid, that's all. But this morning I woke up and thought today's the day."

Oscar once read that when one is sad, he or she seeks out the person whom he or she loves the most because that person will make everything better, or at least a little bit. Upon seeing Anna in his Yale dorm room, he felt an overwhelming surge of grief fill his heart and couldn't help but weep. She held him close, and he rested his head on her shoulder.

"I'm here now. It's OK," she whispered.

She was whom he needed to share in the grief over Sebastian. She was his love, and only she could understand his grief-stricken heart.

They lay together on Oscar's bed. He cried and spoke of Sebastian. He told her what had happened and how sometimes the guilt became so strong that he felt it would consume him.

"I hate myself for not being able to stop him," Oscar said. "I feel like I didn't even know him. He kept everything to himself, and I just wish that he knew he could've told me and that I'd have understood."

"Don't blame yourself, Oz. Coming face to face with who you really are is the scariest thing a person can do," Anna replied. She had a way of putting things in perspective.

She listened to his memories of Sebastian and held him when he slept. When he woke up crying, she consoled him and helped him drift back to sleep. She told him that she'd broken up with Ted after the party. It was wrong of her to ever be with him.

Anna stayed with Oscar over the next few days until it
came time for her to go back to New York. When they
were together, time stood still and nothing outside of
Oscar's dorm room mattered, but eventually, like all
things, reality found a way of catching up with them.
Anna had to be back at school to finish her senior year of
ballet.

On weekends she'd come to New Haven to
visit him, or he'd travel to the city to be with her.

Oscar would often come back to his room to
find Shostakovich's waltz blasting through the
gramophone while his roommates gawked at the
beautiful girl doing a grand battement followed by a
dozen pirouettes. He couldn't be angry with them for
staring; he'd be doing the same if he were in their shoes.
His roommates didn't mind Anna being around, because
she was a fantastic cook and often prepared meals. When
it came time for her to leave, she'd leave Oscar little
notes on his bedroom mirror written in lipstick: *Yours till
the banana splits.* Or *Yours till the goose bumps.* Each one
remained unsmudged until the next.

Another note arrived on his doormat one
Monday morning. Oscar had woken early to drive Anna
to the station so that she'd be back in New York before
her first lesson. He returned back to find a letter with his
name on the envelope written in an all-too-familiar
handwriting. It was from Johnny. Five months too late
but from Johnny nonetheless. Oscar was hesitant. He
took the letter back to his dorm room, locked the door,
and curled up under his duvet.

Dearest Oscar,

I miss you. But not enough to come home. After I left New York, I sailed aimlessly across the waters of the Pacific—drunk. So very, very drunk. I was unable to face up and accept what had happened. I drank so much that I was unable to control the boat, and I crashed into a high reef. I swam to Puerto Vallarta. I've been here ever since. It's the most beautiful place I've ever seen.

I was broken when I got here. I'd finally hit rock bottom and ended up in a hospital. Please don't worry. You know I'm a man of steel. I had to see the darkness so that I could build myself back up.

The time has come for me to use my powers for the greater good, and so I'm joining the US Navy as a naval aviator. War is coming, Oscar. Father and other bigots at Yale may tell you otherwise, but the United States can't stay hidden for much longer. I'm preparing to be prepared.

Until next time,

Johnny

It was short, witty, and to the point, much like all things Johnny Archambault. Oscar couldn't help but feel angry though. He scrunched up the letter and tossed it onto his desk. He'd always seen Johnny as one of the strongest and bravest men he knew. Johnny could take on the world if he had to, but deserting ones family at a time when they needed him most was not a quality that Oscar admired. Johnny was a coward; he was selfish. After months of wishing he'd come home, Oscar decided that maybe Johnny didn't need to. Oscar could manage without him.

CHAPTER 7

It was spring. New life radiated through Central Park as the cherry trees and magnolia blossoms came into bloom. The great lawn was finally getting its light green color back after months of rain and frost. Oscar was in the city to meet with his father. One of Straub's secretaries had called him the week before to make an appointment. He was told to be at the St. Regis Hotel at one o'clock for a luncheon with Straub Archambault. It was overly formal, but that was the only way Straub knew how to operate. He'd not seen Straub since February when his father had turned fifty-five years old. It was a quiet affair, just a meal at Stronghold. Oscar took Anna. Cornelia brought Bennett. She also announced that she was planning on joining the nurses' aid and moving to London. Bennett was a pilot in the US Air Force and would soon be stationed in Cambridgeshire. If she was in London, they'd be closer than if she was in New York. With everyone around him joining the fight, Oscar often weighted his options and thought about signing up as a pilot in the US Air Force. He'd spoken to Anna about it. "When the time comes, you'll know the right thing to do," she said. Cornelia's announcement had just about ruined Straub's birthday meal. He was already furious that Johnny was now a naval aviator serving on an aircraft carrier somewhere in the Pacific.

"It's OK, dear. Soon we'll have no children left," Iris had said while sipping on her sixth martini. She eventually got so emotional that she retired to her bedroom. When Oscar went in to say good-bye, she was sitting in the dark on a chair facing the window. "Does my unhappiness overwhelm you, Oscar?" she asked quietly while lighting a cigarette.

"No, Mother. We all noticed the missing piece at the dinner table," Oscar replied, referring to Sebastian's empty seat, which Iris insisted that no one sit on.

"Don't laugh at me, Oscar. I can't help it. Your father doesn't speak to me."

Oscar knew his mother was unhappy. She hadn't been the same since Sebastian died. She spent Christmas day locked in her bedroom.

"The pain will never go away," he said. "You just have to get used to it. Our lives are different now. We have to start living differently."

"I don't want to!" she shouted.

"Neither do I, but we have no choice," Oscar said softly. He reluctantly rested his hand on Iris's shoulder. Physical contact between the Archambaults was as rare as cats barking.

"You are the one who guards this family now, Oscar." Iris said, forcing a smile. Oscar thought nothing of this comment at the time—Iris often spoke in drunken riddles—but for some reason, this stuck with him, especially as he was on his way to the St. Regis to meet with Straub.

Oscar entered the King Cole bar, a large room with many circular tables in it. Immediately, the host offered to take his Burberry rain coat. Oscar wore a nicely cut navy suit with a grey tie. "I'll show you to your table, Master Archambault." Oscar followed the maître d' towards the far end of the room where Straub was sitting and smoking a cigarette. An expanse of white table cloth draped the table and a half-drunk martini sat in front next to the ashtray. In contrast to Oscar's navy, Straub had opted for his usual double-breasted black suit and red tie.

"Sorry, I'm late," Oscar said as he sat down. The maître d' clicked his fingers to alert one of the young waiters. One quickly rushed over. "May I get you a drink, sir?" He was looking at Oscar.

"Red snapper." Oscar smiled.

The waiter rushed off to the bar. Oscar reached into his pocket and pulled out a crumpled packet of cigarettes. He shook one out and lit it. Straub watched as Oscar clumsily fumbled with the packet.

"The *Yale Daily News* keeping you busy?" Straub asked.

"Very. I get to write about things that matter now. You know, as opposed to my opinions of various cheeses on sale at the on-campus farmers' market," Oscar explained.

"And what is it that matters?" Straub asked.

"Reviews of plays and movies. Last week I wrote a swell piece on *The Cherry Orchard*. I get a whole column now." Oscar was sardonic. The waiter brought his red snapper on a silver tray. Oscar took the half-sliced lemon and squeezed it into the glass before throwing the squished lemon onto the tray for the waiter to take away.

"And you think this stuff is what matters?"

"Of course. People rely on the arts to let their imaginations drift." Oscar stubbed out his cigarette and sipped his cocktail. "Very helpful after a busy week of studying. You should try it sometime."

"I used to go to the opera once a week. And the ballet. Now I don't have time."

"Would you like to hear today's specials, Mr Archambault." The waiter was back and smiling at Straub.

"Give us a moment, would you?" The waiter left. Straub looked at Oscar. "I assume you're wondering why I've asked you here today."

All of a sudden, Oscar began to feel the gentle hum of anxiety. It had been silenced for months; he had almost forgotten what it felt like.

"It's a matter of business, the Archambault business and you."

At that moment, Iris's "one who guards us" comment made sense. Oscar lit himself another cigarette, anything to keep his mind off the anxiety.

"Due to unfortunate circumstances, you are essentially the heir," Straub continued.

"You're forgetting Johnny." Oscar exhaled.

"He's gone. It was never for him."

Oscar wondered what would happen if he left. He and Anna could go and get lost somewhere far, far away. Johnny did it. Sure, he was immersed in guilt, which gave him no other choice but to leave. Oscar's thoughts soon brought him back to reality. He was nothing like Johnny, leaving was not an option for Oscar. He was not one to dissatisfy those who relied upon him. It was a trait he detested, especially at that moment.

"As heir, it is your obligation to take over the business when I retire." Straub looked at Oscar's sullen face. It had never been Oscar's path to take on Archambault Industries. He was third in line to the throne, so he figured it was unlikely that he'd ever get there. This knowledge gave Oscar an option that Sebastian never had, a chance to plan his future the way he wished. He wanted to travel and write about and photograph the astonishing things he would see. His dream to become a top writer for the *National Geographic* seemed to crash all around him.

"I'm going to die soon, Oscar. Archambault Industries will die with me and that will be that," Straub explained pragmatically. "Everything that your grandfather, great-grandfather and great-great-grandfather worked for will be gone. Otto Zombach and his bone-headed son will either run us into the ground or steal all of our assets."

Otto Zombach was on the board of directors at Archambault Industries. He and Straub had known each other since their Yale days, but after thirty-five years of working together, Straub had grown to despise his short, plump, balding board member. Oscar nodded and finished off his red snapper.

"You probably just thought that this was Sebastian's burden?" Straub asked.

"I guess so."

"Life is full of disappointments, son. We just have to get up and carry on." Straub clicked his fingers, and the waiter came rushing over. "We're ready to hear those specials now."

"Of course, Mr Archambault. We have the grilled lamb with roasted grapes. A peppercorn trio of swordfish with cognac sauce..." Oscar stopped listening. He'd lost his appetite. He didn't like to think of Archambault Industries as a burden, because it had given him a very comfortable life. What played on his mind most, much more than sacrificing his *National Geographic* dream, was the realization that if he were to take a seat on the Archambault throne, he would have to give up Anna. He would enter a lifestyle that she loathed. He loved her far too much to allow her to follow him down that path. He knew she was reluctant to end up like her mother. "She was boxed into a life she did not choose nor did she want it," Anna would say. She always feared that if she were to meet the same fate, the dark thoughts would enter her mind, and she too would kill herself.

He decided not to mention anything to Anna or to anyone else. Straub's plan was for Oscar to finish the remaining two years of Yale he had left and then begin at Archambault Industries. By then Anna hoped to be in London with the Royal Ballet or Paris with the opera ballet. She had plans, none of which involved Oscar. He'd always known that but hoped they'd find a way. He knew that if he asked her to stay, she would, but he'd never forgive himself and, eventually, neither would she.

The next few months were occupied by the preparation of Estella's marriage to Lane Hamilton. Anna was to be one of six bridesmaids. She and Oscar had received a joint invitation, which made Oscar feel a little bit like he was going as a bridesmaid's plus one rather than the bride's brother.

Straub and Iris Archambault
invite you to celebrate the marriage of their
daughter

Estella Rose
to
Lane Everett Hamilton

son of Wade and Patricia Hamilton

on Saturday, the sixth of April, nineteen forty
at two in the afternoon.
St. Patrick's Cathedral, Fifth Avenue, New York,
New York

The wedding was a grand affair. Not even the news of Winston Churchill becoming prime minister could take the spotlight off Estella Archambault on her big day. After the wedding, Oscar and Anna retired to his bedroom at the Archambault townhouse. They made love, and Anna fell asleep not long after. She was tired from the busy day and had to be up and ready to catch a nine o'clock train to Boston in the morning. She had an audition with the Moscow Ballet. They were putting on a production of *Sleeping Beauty*. Oscar had lied by telling her that he'd be gone in the morning because his train back to New Haven was earlier. He sat at his desk watching her sleep and thinking about whether lying to her had been the right thing to do. He felt an awful pang of guilt over it. He pulled a piece of paper from his top desk drawer and took his fountain pen from the wooden box near the lamp.

Dear Anna,

Before I start, I want you to know that this isn't a good-bye letter. This is for all the words left unsaid between us. This is for all the moments that are forever held in our memories. This is for treasuring the past and embracing the future.

I remember the first day you came to Stronghold. I looked at you and told Sebastian that I thought you were an angel. I've thought that every time I have seen you since —even now as I look at you sleeping peacefully in my bed. When you kissed me at the Bethesda fountain, I did not know how I got to be so lucky. I could not believe that it was me you picked to hold your heart. I made a promise to you and to myself that I'd remind you how honoured I am every day that you chose me. Regrettably with this vow comes a hindrance, which is that I must put you and your feelings before mine. By default, I have become heir to my father's business. My place is at Archambault tower. The only way we can work is by my holding you back from fulfilling the greatness that is within you. I only want you to be happy, and I'm sorry that it can't be with me. If two people are meant to be together, eventually they'll find their way back to one another. I hope that one day, in the not too distant future, I'll pass you in the street, and we'll rent a boat and float on the lake like we did last summer. You'll tell me of all your adventures. This is not good-bye; it's see you later. Live your life. Don't let anything hold you back.

Yours till the tree barks,

Oz

Oscar folded the letter and placed it in the front pocket of Anna's bag. He then slid into bed next to her and held her until the time came for him to get up and leave, knowing that he'd lose her heart and unsure whether she would ever be able to forgive him.

THE END

ABOUT THE AUTHOR

Sarah Lee is a self-published author from Birmingham, England. Though she's written short stories and screenplays for as long as she can remember, *The Gentle Hum of Anxiety* is her first novel. After writing, photography is her greatest passion. She works with dogs and enjoys taking pictures of their silly antics.

14518190R10054

Printed in Great Britain
by Amazon.co.uk, Ltd.,
Marston Gate.